Snow Ordinary Love

Chris Walters

Also by
Chris Walters

The Tashaverse:
No One Like You
Make It Real
Send Me An Angel

Other Books:
Goddess Good
In The Slot

ISBN: 978-1-964292-02-1

eBook ISBN: 978-1-964292-05-2

Visit the link below to listen to the Snow Ordinary Love playlist.

This book is dedicated to every person with the empathy, kindness, and decency to see others as their neighbors and treat them with love, regardless of the color of their skin, their gender, or their sexuality, AND who also has the courage and the vision to extend that love around the globe. No person should be considered less than because of where they were born, or whom they were born to.

People are people. Love is love.

Preface
Content Awareness

This book is a contemporary monster romance set in the modern United States. In this fictional reality, the USA experimented with teleportation in the 1980s, bringing orcs and elves into our world. Elves, being tall, thin, and fair, were immediately granted citizenship. Orcs were not. In case the dedication wasn't a big enough hint, there are some strong allegories to the caste society of the USA and the mistreatment of non-citizens. The romance in is this book is definitely open door. There are also brief mentions of sex work.

Contents

Chapter 1

Saturday Night's Alright (For Fighting)

Elton John

Mona flinched when the bottle shattered against the back of her skull, beer and backwash running down her ponytail and tattooed back. Her arms relaxed, allowing the human in her grasp to stagger forward before she kicked him in the back of the knee. He collapsed to the sticky floor with a sickening pop as Mona wheeled to face his moron friend with the beer bottle. The gibbering idiot blanched as her lips peeled back to reveal her mandibular fangs. Ebony ink rippled over emerald skin as Mona flexed her muscles. Her grin widened when she saw him grip the broken neck of the bottle, glistening shards pointed at her abdomen.

"I see a deadly weapon in your hand," Mona announced in a voice pitched for the entire room to hear over the blaring hip-hop. The human male glanced uncertainly at the broken bottle in his hand. Adrenaline flooded her arteries as the young idiot in front of her swung the sharp glass wildly. Mona allowed his momentum to carry him forward, grasping his outstretched arm to pull him along. Overbalanced, the human stumbled along until his solar plexus met her rising knee. The impact stalled his body's motion, but his arm—aided by her firm grip—continued forward until his shoulder popped audibly. Nearby patrons winced visibly at the sound.

Glass fell from nerveless fingers to crash on the floor, followed by their former wielder, who clutched his ruined arm in a breathless scream. Glaring around the room, Mona shouted, "Do *not* touch the fucking dancers."

At her feet, the older of the two humans whimpered as he inched away from her, his twisted leg extended behind him while his companion struggled to comprehend the shock of the injury to his shoulder. Silently, Mona named the first one, Knees, and the other one, Shoulders. She gripped the neck of Knees in one hand and the shirt of Shoulders in the other and dragged them toward the door. Throwing the pair of injured humans onto the pavement, Mona turned on her heel to walk back inside when Knees shouted at her.

"Do you know who I am? You're fucking finished, you green *bitch.*"

I've heard the same thing a thousand times before, you worthless sheep fucker. These shitlickers see an orc and they figure they're all smarter, classier, and overall better *than me because their skin isn't green. I hate this fucking job.*

She strolled back into the club as the idiot with the busted shoulder finally recovered enough oxygen to begin wailing. Tiffany winked at her from the stage as she started her set. Mona kept half an eye on her friend as Tiffany tugged at the tie of her schoolgirl outfit, pulling it between her teeth to cheers from the audience. The assembled humans and elves voiced their approval as Tiffany's clothes came off, one by one. Mona made sure they kept their hands mostly to themselves as they stuffed cash into the stripper's garter belt. For some reason, watching someone get their ass kicked always seemed to supercharge the audience's collective libido. Mona was happy her friend was the beneficiary of their overhyped largesse.

Once the club's doors closed and the patrons all stumbled off to wherever they came from, Mona was summoned to the manager's office. The Devil's Playground wasn't owned and operated by an *actual* devil, demon, or other infernal fiend from the Abyssal pits, but Gus was about as close as it got. The foul human grinned at her as he barked, "Close the door, Mona." Once closed, he motioned for her to approach his desk. In a voice oozing condescension and overwrought concern, he said, "It seems we have a situation. A very *sticky* situation, indeed."

Fighting down the urge to roll her eyes, Mona stared at him, waiting for him to continue.

He emitted a disappointed huff before going on, "Those two guys you bounced earlier. The one who is going to be walking funny for weeks is a city councilman. As for the kid with the fucked up shoulder, that's the councilman's son. This is gonna bring unnecessary heat down on us. I'm afraid I'm gonna have to let you go...unless you convince me otherwise." His grin turned lecherous as he stroked his groin.

"I'm not fucking you to keep this shitty job."

"Too bad. I was hoping to see if you were a moaner, Mona."

Ooh, so clever. You're only the ten thousandth person to ever come up with such an unoriginal thought.

"Sorry to disappoint you, Gus."

No, I'm not.

"I'm going to have to dock your pay, though. To cover damages, you see."

Mona kept her voice to a tightly-reined growl and flexed her hands to keep from balling them into fists. "Are you fucking kidding me?"

"Well, you took fucking off the table, but if you blow me I might give you half pay." He must have surmised the answer by the expression on her face because he hastily added, "Don't even think of hurting me. If you lay a finger on me, I'll guarantee you never work in Portland again. Leave now, peacefully, and I won't blackball your orc ass."

Mona resisted the urge to break his neck and instead turned on her heel. The walls shook as she slammed the office door closed behind her. Tiffany trotted out of the club after her, clad now in sweatpants and a university hoodie. "Hey. Mona. Wait up."

She came to a halt to allow her friend to catch up. "Mona, are you okay?"

"No, I just got fucking fired, and fucking Gus is stealing all of my pay for so-called damages. It's fucking horseshit."

"I'm sorry, hon," Tiffany said with a wan smile. The bridge of her nose crinkled as she grimaced. "He's *such* an asshole."

Mona grunted in response, not willing to face her friend because she felt tears welling in her eyes. "I hated this job, but it's not like I have a lot of opportunities."

"I know. It sucks, and I'm sorry."

"Do you know? You're a human, you have options. People save the worst possible jobs for orcs. Bouncing was about as good as it gets for me. Now I can't even pay rent for my shitty basement apartment."

"You could move in with me." Tiffany slid her arms around Mona's chest.

"I appreciate the offer, Tiff, but we both know Flora would never allow an orc under her roof." Flora was Tiffany's elven landlady and made her displeasure manifestly apparent anytime Mona came around. She could feel the tears sliding down her cheeks as she contemplated her extremely limited options. "What am I going to do?"

"Sweetie, I wish I knew."

Mona rotated in Tiffany's arms until she ended up hugging her friend. They held each other in the parking lot, Mona resting her head on Tiffany's shoulder with her eyes closed until she felt a nudge. Tiffany's nose tapped against her chin, so Mona raised her head off her friend's shoulder. Her eyes flew open when her friend's lips met her own. Without thinking, she kissed Tiffany back, lips opening to allow tongues to dance and trace each other's teeth.

What the fuck am I doing? Stop kissing her. Okay, maybe a little more. No, Mona, you need to stop.

Mona separated her lips from Tiffany's and pressed her friend back. "Tiff, why?"

"Don't overthink it, Mona. You're in pain, and I want to help you take the edge off."

"But..." Her thoughts moved at the speed of a slug.

"I'm sorry if I overstepped. My best friend was hurting, and it felt right in the moment." She grinned mischievously. "Plus, I've been told that I'm a good kisser." The grin faded a bit. "Seriously though, I hope I didn't freak you out."

Mona inhaled deeply and held the air in her lungs as she willed her racing heart to slow down. A long exhale preceded her response. "Tiff, thank you so much. I appreciate your desire to help, I..." Her voice trailed off as her mind struggled to express herself while not upsetting her friend.

Tiffany smiled at her under glittering blue eyes, but held her silence.

She's my friend. My best friend. She'll understand.

"I love you more than I can say. Every day, I am grateful you came up to me eating lunch alone in the first grade and had the courage to sit and talk with me when no one else would. Our relationship means everything to me, and I don't want to complicate things between us. Having you hug me and listen is everything I need."

Through the misty veil of her own vision, Mona could see tears glimmering on her friend's cheeks. "Thank you, Mona. You'll always be my best friend, and I'm *not* looking to upgrade our status." Tiff flashed her a wink and tittered as she pawed at her tears. "At least come home with me. You're having a shit time, and tonight will be better if you're not sleeping alone."

"What about Flora?"

"Flora can fuck off," Tiffany snorted. "She can take her stuck-up attitude and shove it up her virginal elvish ass."

Mona snickered. "If you say so. I'll follow you back to your place."

"Cool, see you there."

Tiffany slid into the front seat of her little electric car and hummed off down the road while Mona strapped her helmet on. Flinging one leg over the seat of her motorcycle, she twisted the ignition and savored the rumble of the engine between her thighs. Checking the road for traffic, she gunned the engine and drove after her friend. After a short drive, they arrived at Tiffany's place. The two-story house soared above them as cold drizzle began to fall.

The walkway was lined with flowering plants which bloomed no matter the season under Flora's care. A thick hedge of rose bushes hemmed the house, providing a lovely view in the daylight, but an effectively thorny deterrent to burglars and lusty paramours in the night. Mona often wondered which threat the elf worried about more.

Jogging up to the entrance, Tiffany fumbled briefly with the key before opening the door. The house was quiet as they stealthily made their way to Tiffany's room on the second floor. Mona's nose twitched at the heavy, cloying scent of potpourri in the air.

Flora must be the most noseblind elf ever. I know the rent is fairly cheap, especially for Portland, but I have no idea how Tiff lives in this nauseating miasma.

Once inside Tiffany's room, Mona fidgeted with the zipper on her jacket as her friend stripped naked. Her movements were efficient and functional, as opposed to the far more alluring performances she put on nightly. Hers was one of two rooms in the boarding house with a private bathroom, which Tiffany entered. She looked over her shoulder at Mona, asking, "Are you just going to stand there, or are you going to get ready for bed?"

"Aren't you going to wear something?"

"Why? You see me naked every night, and it's not like I've never seen you naked. Quit being a baby and take your clothes off. I have a spare toothbrush if you want."

"Tiff, I thought I was clear about not having sex."

Those blue eyes locked on her own, framed by arched eyebrows. "I'm well aware. I'll keep my hands to safe zones, tempting as you are." Tiffany grinned and stuck her tongue out. "Skin-to-skin contact will help you feel better. Trust me on this, I'm an expert." With a wink, she added, "I won't be offended if you keep your underwear on. It'll make resisting you much easier."

Chuckling to herself, Mona fumbled with buttons and straps as she disrobed before padding into the bathroom to brush her teeth with the proffered toothbrush. Once done, she joined Tiffany under the thick blankets.

"Damn. Your sheets are amazing." They felt soft and slick against her bare skin.

Tiffany tittered. "One of the few luxuries I permit myself. Now roll over onto your side. Facing away from me."

She complied. Tiffany's skin felt warm, in contrast with the cool sheets, as she molded herself to Mona's back and legs. One arm snaked over her torso, and their fingers intermingled on her stomach.

"Mona?"

"Yeah?"

"I'm sorry about Gus, losing your job, and all the shit you have to deal with. I'll always be here for you, no matter what."

"Thanks, Tiff. It means a lot to me."

"I've got you. If you need to talk now we can. Otherwise, get some sleep and we'll talk later."

Mona grunted and closed her eyes.

She's right. Contact and physical touch does make me feel better.

A knock on the door woke her hours later. As her mind fought to ascend from the depths of slumber, she registered her condition. She was sweaty and hot under the blankets and could feel Tiffany's hand cupping a boob. The gentle snoring in her ear morphed into snorting when there was another knock.

A high-pitched voice beyond the door shouted, "Tiffany, I see that greenie's bike out back. You better not have brought an orc into this house."

Mona felt her blood simmering, burning away the vestiges of sleep. Before she could respond, Tiffany called out, "Fuck off, Flora.

Mona had a bad night and she stayed with me. She's not going to drive your precious property value down because she slept here once."

Flora's voice went up a couple octaves into an undignified screech. "You can't speak to me in such a crude manner."

"Go trim your bushes or something. Leave us alone."

Mona heard Flora stomp off, or at least an elf's best attempt at a stomp.

"Mmm, you've got great tits." Tiffany punctuated her murmur with a gentle squeeze, which sent a rush of blood to Mona's groin.

It's time to get moving before my pussy starts thinking for me. Right now, she's reminding me just how long it's been since she's seen anything but my fingers and toys, and I'm starting to find the argument compelling.

Mona gently pulled Tiffany's hand off her breast and down to her stomach. "I should go so you don't get in more shit with Flora."

"Stay a bit longer."

"Tiff..."

Her friend peeled herself away and sat up in bed, sheets and blankets pooled around her lap. "Fine," she grumped, her expression slumping into a pout. "Did sleeping here help at least?"

"It did. Thank you. I feel surprisingly better, even if life still sucks grizzly bear balls."

Tiffany snickered. "Lovely image." Her expression suddenly brightened. "Speaking of grizzly bears, I just had a thought."

"Oh?"

"Why don't you go up to my brother's cabin for a few days? He always keeps it stocked, and he's down in Phoenix with his wife. It's isolated, you can meditate in peace, and figure out whatever your next steps will be."

"I don't know."

"Look, whatever issues you have with my brother are with him, not a cabin in the mountains."

"Issues" is underselling things a bit, but I never told you the full truth, either.

"What about the weather? There's another atmospheric river coming."

"It's just rain. You'll be fine."

"Okay. I'll do it."

Tiffany's face lit up again as she leaned in for a hug. "It'll be great, I promise."

"I'm not so sure, but you're right. A change of scenery will be helpful, and I do love the mountains."

She could feel Tiffany's boobs pressed against her when her friend asked, "Speaking of mountains, I'm still thinking of waking up with your tits in my hand. Are we one hundred percent sure about the 'friends with no benefits' thing?"

Mona laughed and gently pushed her back. "My tits aren't mountainous. They're barely foothills. One hundred percent? No. Call it ninety-nine percent. Either way, I'm not fucking you, even though I'm certain it would be a great time for both of us."

Tiffany mock pouted before bounding out of bed to her dresser. Mona was certain she popped her ass out more than necessary in her search for the keys to her brother's cabin, but Mona was unmoved.

Girl, I've seen your goods on display for years now. I always enjoy the show, but you're not going to tempt me.

"Found 'em." Tiffany whirled, keys held in the air triumphantly.

"Thanks," Mona said as she slid out of bed and began putting on her clothes.

"Have you considered stripping? You've got the body for it."

"Come on, Tiff. We've talked about this. You know what kind of clubs allow orc strippers. I don't want to be abused and degraded every night."

"What if we went independent? You and I. We could strip for parties and stuff."

"I don't think so."

Tiffany sat down next to her on the bed and held one of her hands. "Well, if nothing else, think about starting an OnlyFeet account." She kicked her legs out and wiggled her toes in the air. "I make a ton of money there, and I bet you could, too. There's a bunch of guys who absolutely worship orc feet. We could do some joint videos in a bathtub to help you build your audience. Trust me, you'll be a hit."

Mona stared at her spinach-colored feet, comparing them to Tiffany's. "My feet look huge, especially compared to yours."

"They're a little bigger than mine, which makes sense since you're taller than me, and an orc to boot." She snickered. "To boot...I didn't mean to make a joke."

"Haha. Very funny." Mona sighed as she reached down to put on her Doc Martens. "While I am up at the cabin, I will *consider* starting an OnlyFeet account. I'll have plenty of stuff to think about."

"If you do, you won't regret it. I promise."

Tiffany threw on a robe to walk Mona out. Along the way, they passed Flora. The icy blonde elf glared at them as they walked by, her eyes staring daggers into Mona's back.

I'm not going to flip her off for Tiff's sake, even if the stuck-up elven bitch deserves it.

Chapter 2

Here I Go Again
Whitesnake

Mona's motorcycle roared as the highway climbed into the Cascade mountain range, the cold December air occasionally worming its way into gaps in her clothing. Drizzling rain evolved into drifting powdery snow as the elevation increased. She kept her speed moderate and stayed within the lanes.

I'm not taking stupid chances, especially in the snow and without a job. Getting there alive is better than the alternatives. It's not like I'm on a schedule.

A while later, Mona turned onto a gravel path, easing her bike along at low speed. The snow fell heavier now and was beginning to stick on the ground. Anxiety built in Mona's veins as her bike's headlight pierced the wintry darkness. She felt a surge of relief when the log cabin appeared in the light ahead.

Mona parked behind a tarp-covered woodpile and dismounted gingerly. She'd been too busy for long rides in recent months and her legs were cramped and stiff after the trip. She trudged up the stairs with her gear and unlocked the door. The inside of the cabin was dark and cold, but she quickly located the lantern exactly where Tiffany's notes said it would be. Switching it on, her eyes adjusted to the pale illumination. She stomped on the doormat to dislodge the light dusting of snow on her boots before striding across the room to the wood stove. She opened it up to see wood and tinder inside, exactly as Tiff predicted. Locating a long match, she set the tinder alight and settled back on her haunches to watch the fire spread.

Once she was sure the logs had caught fire, she closed the gate and stood. The hardwood walls of the cabin gave it a rustic charm, complemented by vintage logging tools hung along the walls. Mona strode over to a window and pulled back the floral print linen curtains. Outside, the snow was still falling. She brushed her fingertips along the edge of the windowpane, noting the lack of draft.

Joel may be a dickhead, but he knows good work. These curtains are definitely his wife's idea, though.

Opening her jacket, she pulled out the printed instructions from Tiffany. Out the back door, she found the generator and fired it up. She noted the hot tub on the deck before checking the well and opening the pipes. Water and power taken care of, she filled and covered the hot tub and got it warming.

A good soak in the morning is going to feel amazing. I can relax and read a book tonight, then hopefully get a good night's sleep. Thank you, Tiffany, for suggesting this.

The air inside the cabin was already warming when she walked in. Mona ran through the rest of the checklist before settling into a comfortable chair with a book and a blanket. She listened to the wind in the trees as she read, letting herself relax.

Mona threw off the blanket after a couple hours and adjusted the wood stove. She took the opportunity to eat some instant mac and cheese she found in Joel's well-organized pantry before settling back in her chair wearing just shorts and a tank top.

Lifting her feet in the air, she checked them out, wiggling her green toes.

I'm pretty sure I won't make a living from OnlyFeet, but some extra money wouldn't hurt. I don't necessarily understand it, but hey, if someone wants to pay good money for photos and videos of my feet, then who am I to deny them?

She read for another hour before she realized she was reading the same paragraph over and over again as she struggled not to nod off. Taking this as a hint, Mona fed more wood into the stove and turned off most of the lights. She climbed the wooden spiral staircase into the loft and pulled sheets and blankets from a small linen closet to make the bed. Turning off the last light, she slid underneath the blankets and quickly fell asleep.

Morning light streaming in from a gap in the curtains woke Mona from her slumber. Her body ached slightly from the unfamiliar bed, and her mouth felt dry and tacky. After gingerly descending the stairs, she padded over to the fireplace to add another split log. She listened to it crackle before grabbing a glass of water to alleviate the gross feeling in her mouth.

Mona found a spot far enough from the wood stove where the heat was only beginning to reach and dropped to the floor for push-ups, followed by crunches. She pulled resistance bands from her bags to work some additional muscle groups. Mona finished off with some yoga to maintain her flexibility.

I should take a quick shower and check on the road in. If I can get into town to buy a few groceries, then I'll be in good shape. An orc can live on instant mac and cheese, but some variety would be better. Maybe I can cook some chili while I relax in the hot tub. Mmm, chili mac would be delicious. And salad. I think I saw a steamer basket. Maybe I can pick up broccoli or cauliflower. All right, Mona. You have a motorcycle. Don't get carried away. You also need to fit a couple six-packs of beer on your bike, too. Preferably something local. Breakfast and coffee in town would be good, too.

She returned a few hours later, satiated and laden with groceries. After packing the small refrigerator, she fixed a batch of chili. Mona grinned as she gazed out the back window to the partially covered deck.

I wish I'd brought a bikini or bought one while I was out, but what the hell. There's no one here to see me anyway.

Mona felt a wave of giddily irreverent energy in her soul as she stripped naked in the middle of the cabin. Piling her clothes on the chair, she checked the wood stove and the chili, grabbed a beer, then scurried out the backdoor. Cold air washed across her warm skin like a thousand Lilliputian daggers. Her skin and nipples pebbled in the frigid atmosphere, and her soles protested as they slapped onto snow-dusted planks. Resting her beer on the picnic table, she hastily yanked the cover off the hot tub. Her prickly limbs ached at the sight of the warm water.

Snatching her beer, Mona swung her legs over the side and into the balmy depths. The rest of her body followed, sinking into the steaming reservoir. "Mmm," she moaned, savoring the heat soothing her skin after her frigid jaunt.

"I know the return trip is going to be even worse, but I'm going to enjoy every minute until then." She laid her head back against the side of the hot tub, letting her auburn and black hair float in a lazy penumbra around her neck. "*Fuck.* I forgot to get a towel out. Oh well."

The only answer to her monologue was the gentle rustling of pine needles in the breeze and the burbling of the hot tub. Mona felt her tension ebbing from her body into the water as she sipped her beer and watched scattered snowflakes drift down. She held herself still when she observed a rabbit dart across the fresh snow from one clump of bushes to another.

I feel a bit like a bunny. Never safe, never secure. Darting from one thing to the next while hoping all the while not to get consumed by a hostile world. Here in the so-called "Land of Opportunity" and "Home of the Free" my options are constrained because I'm an orc. I'd call myself a second-class citizen, but I'm not even a citizen. I'm a refugee from a world I've never seen and may no longer even exist. Of course, the elves were granted citizenship, but not the orcs. Elves are tall, thin, beautiful, elegant, and charming, and orcs are just tall.

When we sued for our rights under the Fourteenth Amendment, the useless Supreme Court ruled it didn't apply to orcs because no orcs lived in this country in 1869. Fucking racist assholes. Of course we weren't here. It wasn't until Ronald Reagan's Star Wars program in the 1980s experimented with teleportation and temporarily opened up gates to my parents' dying world.

Mona shook her head to clear her mind before the negativity spiraled any further. She chugged the rest of her beer and levered herself out of the tub. The rivulets of warm water running down her limbs cooled quickly in the frigid air. "Fuck, fuck, fuck," she swore as she hastily covered the hot tub and fled for the cabin door as her skin pebbled once again.

Slamming the door behind her, she raced for the wood stove. She basked in the heat and rotated her body slowly like meat on a spit. It took her five full rotations to feel the last of the chill evaporate. Once warmed, she grabbed a towel and dried whatever droplets the stove missed. She soaked up the small puddle on the floor before hanging the towel on a drying rack.

I should get dressed and check my chili. Actually, should *I get dressed? It's not like there's anyone here but me. Society's silly rules don't apply up here in the mountains. Honestly, what has society ever done for me except tell me I wasn't good enough, smart enough, or capable enough? It's time for me to stop letting society constrain my choices.*

Mona relished her newfound sense of freedom as she strode over to the kitchenette. She put a pan of rice on the stove as she stirred her chili, inhaling the spicy aroma. After lunch, she settled into the chair by the wood stove with her book and a light blanket for an afternoon of reading and relaxing.

She tugged on clothes briefly to collect wood from the woodpile to restock the stove before the sun set. While outside, she covered her motorcycle with a tarp, noting the fresh snowfall.

I hope Tiff was right about the atmospheric river. If it's this cold when the rain hits, then I could be in for a shitload of snow. At least I have a good amount of food, a working generator, and plenty of wood. And a hot tub. I should do another soak before dinner.

Not long after, Mona was once again basking in the balmy depths of the hot tub.

All right. It's time to start thinking of my next steps. I'll do the OnlyFeet thing. Tiff mentioned striking out on her own, stripping at parties and such. I could be her muscle, but I'm not sure how well such a business would do in the strip club capital of the U.S. What I want to do is start a frozen yogurt shop. I'm tired of bouncing, security, and generally being a goon for hire. FroYo would be fun, creative, and I don't think the market is completely saturated. Even better would be a FroYo truck. Lower startup costs, although storage might be an issue. The problem is getting a loan. Banks don't like lending to orcs.

Before she could get caught in a spiral of negativity again, Mona leaned back against the side of the tub and did her breathing exercises. She concentrated on the rhythm of her lungs and the feel of the water against her skin. Finding serenity took patience, but she eventually claimed her center. As her body relaxed and the hot tub's jets tickled and caressed her skin, Mona felt a giddy rush of arousal. She let herself drift, savoring the boundary between hot and cold, relaxation and arousal. In her gauzy state of repose, she observed the snow coming down harder. The dying rays of late afternoon sunlight were almost completely obscured by a cloak of swirling whiteness.

"Damn," she muttered to herself as reality intruded and rudely banished her zen state. "It looks like I'm in for a blizzard tonight. I need to check on the generator, which means I need clothes. All right, Mona. Time to haul ass inside."

She was psyching herself up for the brief, yet frigid dash from the hot tub to the cabin when she heard what sounded like a slamming car door. The noise jolted her into motion. Scuttling out of the slippery tub, she threw on the cover quickly and grabbed her beer before bolting to the cabin.

Mona closed the door behind her and took a single shivering and soaking step forward when the cabin's front door swung open, revealing a man standing uncertainly in the open doorway.

"What the fuck are *you* doing here?" she shouted.

"Me? What are *you* doing here? And why are you naked?" He shouted back.

Suddenly very aware of her state of undress, Mona strangled the urge to cover herself and instead willed herself to stand up straighter. "Tiffany said I could use the cabin for a few days. Speaking of...where's your wife?"

She could see the corners of his blue eyes twitch and his lips tighten. His voice was flat as he responded, "Cheri isn't coming."

"Well, close the damn door, then."

Joel had the grace to look abashed as he kicked the door closed behind him.

Mona opened her mouth to ask another question when a plaintive cry interrupted her. "Joel, what was—" She belatedly noted the tote in his left hand wasn't a gym bag as she first thought, but was actually a carrier. Another plaintive cry erupted from the bag.

"Do you mind?" Joel nodded his head toward the carrier.

"Are you stupid? Let the poor thing out."

She regarded Joel as he knelt to set down the soft-sided carrier. His gloved hands fumbled awkwardly with the zipper.

"Idiot," Mona hissed under her breath as she strode across the room. She dropped to her knees and brushed Joel's hands away, cognizant of the glorious vista she was gifting him. The baleful bawling ceased when she slid the zipper open and a fluffy head appeared. Two golden eyes stared at Mona before a huge tabby cat shot out of the carrier and hid under a chair.

Mona glanced up to observe Joel's gaze locked solidly on her, not the cat.

"Enjoying the view?" She asked with a sardonic twist in her voice.

His face flushed scarlet at being caught. Joel twisted his neck to force his vision elsewhere. Staring pointedly at the wall, he stammered a response, "Could...could you maybe put on some clothes?"

Her sneer was wasted on his ear. Twirling around, she strutted toward the spiral stairs. The sneer remained as she ascended.

Enjoy the view, asshole. It's all you're going to get.

Up in the loft, Mona's heart thundered in her chest. Her hands felt clammy as she clenched and unclenched them while she paced. Seeing Joel after so many years brought with it a rampaging horde of emotions which she struggled to process.

Once I get dressed, I need to find a way to get rid of him if the weather permits. I came up here for serenity, and Joel's presence is the antithesis of peace and quiet. My goal is to figure out my path forward and he is nothing but my past—a past I want to keep far in my rearview. Why didn't Tiff tell me he was coming? Is she trying to pull some kind of trick on me? And of course, what kind of sick joke of the Goddess is it that the first time he sees me in forever, I'm not wearing a stitch of clothing?

She pulled on sweatpants, a hoodie, and shoes while her mind tried to focus on the problem at hand. Mona grunted as she stood. Descending the stairs, she observed Joel kneeling on the floor and whispering to the cat underneath the chair.

"I'm checking the generator, and then we'll talk."

He mumbled something unintelligible as she walked toward the back door. Outside in the frigid air, the generator hummed along in the darkness. Mona checked the fuel level and made sure no snow was getting into the enclosure around the generator. Satisfied the power would stay on, she briefly observed the heavily falling snow before she returned to the warmth of the cabin.

Joel held the cat in one arm as he fumbled with the carrier with the other. He struggled as the cat attempted to worm its way out of his grasp.

"What are you doing?" she asked.

"You somehow got up here without a car, so I'm trying to get Bitsy into her carrier, and then we're leaving."

"How bad were the conditions coming in?"

"Awful, but—"

"No. *You* can leave if you want, but your cat stays here. I don't want you killing an innocent creature because you're a flaming idiot."

Bitsy leapt out of Joel's arms when he stiffened in shock. The massive feline scampered back under the chair and hissed at Joel when he took a step toward her.

"See? The cat is clearly smarter than you." Mona noted Joel's grimace before continuing. "Not a particularly high bar to clear, but hey."

"Fuck off, Mona. What did I ever do to you?"

"You mean beside fucking me and then ghosting me?"

His tanned skin bloomed red like a chrysanthemum in the summer heat from his neck up to the scalp under his thinning comb-over. "We were teenagers."

"You told me you loved me, you worthless asshole. Then after I handed you my virginity on a silver platter, you never talked to me again. I don't give a shit what age we were. There's no excuse for treating anyone the way you treated me."

"I'm sorry, Mona."

He looked mildly apologetic but mostly embarrassed.

Mona grimaced before delivering a sarcastic retort. "Well, thanks, Joel. Saying 'I'm sorry' fifteen years later definitely fixes everything."

"Really?" he asked hopefully.

"No, you idiot. Your crappy apology doesn't change shit," she snarled. Mona could feel the accumulated calm of the past day fading rapidly as her blood heated. Even worse, she felt the tips of her mandibular fangs poking past her lips.

Great, now I'm flashing fang like a fucking barbarian, thereby reinforcing every negative stereotype about orcs and our so-called primitive nature. It's a handy crowd control trick for a bouncer, but a pain in my ass when I'm arguing with my best friend's asshole brother.

Joel's face was blotchy, and his hands balled into fists before he shook them out. "What are you doing here anyway, Mona? This is my cabin."

"Thanks for the reminder, Captain Obvious. Way to lord your capitalist privilege over the working class orc." Mona sneered as Joel blanched. "Since you asked, I bounced a city councilman a couple nights ago after he and his dipshit son got handsy with one of the dancers. He got pissy about it, so my asshole boss fired me. Tiff suggested I come up here to clear my head and figure shit out." Mona paused to regard Joel carefully. "She didn't tell you?"

"No." Joel shook his head. "She didn't know I was coming."

"Yeah. Aren't you supposed to be in Phoenix...with your wife?"

"It's none of your business," Joel responded gruffly, his face going blotchy red again.

"Hang on..." A grin spread across Mona's face as realization dawned. "You're a thousand miles away from home, with your cat, and your sister doesn't know you're here. Holy shit, your wife kicked your ass out."

"That's not...it was mutual," he mumbled.

"You both mutually kicked your ass out?" She couldn't keep the giddiness from her voice.

His hands balled into fists again. "*Fuck you,* bitch. You're fucking trespassing, so don't make me kick your ass out into the snow."

Mona sneered and flexed her tattooed arm muscles. "Bring it, bitch-boy." She assessed Joel, just in case he tried to get physical. He was taller than she was, but not by much. His arms indicated some muscle mass from the gym or physical labor, but he wasn't well-toned. Joel's heaving torso indicated a lack of conditioning. He wasn't fat, but he didn't appear to be in fighting shape, either. She liked her chances in a fight.

They stood still, glaring at each other until Joel's shoulders slumped as he unclenched his fists. "I'm sorry. It's been a rough week, and I wasn't expecting you to be here...I shouldn't have snapped at you. This isn't your problem. Tiffany said you could come up here, and I'm sure you'd rather be alone, so I'll just go."

She rolled her eyes. "Stop being dramatic. Unless the snow stopped, you're not going anywhere and we both know it. Right now, let's get your shit out of your car. Then I want you to introduce me to your furry little friend. Bitsy, is it?"

"Yeah, Bitsy. She's a good girl."

They trudged out into the snowy darkness. The snowfall was heavy enough to mostly obscure the cabin from the car. Joel piled a litter box and a couple bags of groceries into Mona's arms. She walked toward the faint halos of light which marked the location of the cabin, gingerly making her way up the short staircase. It took three trips for them to get everything he needed from the vehicle.

Mona put the final bag down with audible clinks. Peering inside, she exclaimed, "*Holy shit, Joel*. Is there any booze left in the store?"

"Very funny. I had to buy all their whiskey because apparently you bought all their beer," he retorted with a nod toward the six pack on the counter.

"Suck it. I bought a couple of six packs. Hardly their whole stock."

"Whatever. Anyway, I was planning to use the hot tub tomorrow, but I'm assuming by your earlier state of undress it's already hot."

"Yes, it is."

He grinned as he waved a bottle of whiskey. "Want to join me?"

"For whiskey or the hot tub?"

Joel shrugged. "Either one." The corners of his mouth twitched lecherously as he added, "both."

"Fuck off. I didn't bring a bikini, and there's no way in hell I'm skinny dipping with you." She saw him open his mouth and forestalled him with a scowl. "And if you say you've already seen everything, I swear I'll shove that whiskey bottle so far up your ass you'll have to reach into your mouth to unscrew it."

He wisely closed his mouth.

"Now introduce me to Bitsy."

"Fine."

"Stop being grumpy."

They both knelt down next to the chair Bitsy was hiding under. "Hey, Bitsy. This is Mona. Mona, this is Bitsy. She's a Maine Coon."

Bitsy poked her head out tentatively. Mona slowly extended a hand to scratch the cat's head. A low rumbling purr reached her ears as Bitsy slowly crawled out from under the chair.

"She's huge. And fluffy. *So* fluffy."

"She weighs about sixteen pounds."

"You're a chonky girl," Mona cooed. "Yes, you are. Yes, you are. And you have such a sweet purr. What's a nice girl like you doing with a total dipshit like Joel? You're a good girl, aren't you?"

"Well, I'm gonna leave you to get acquainted while I go sit in the hot tub."

"Uh-huh."

Mona kept scratching and murmuring to Bitsy until she heard the back door close. She levered herself up from the floor and ascended the stairs. Slipping into more comfortable shorts and a tank top, she returned downstairs and curled into a chair by the wood stove with a book. Bitsy hopped up into her lap and quickly settled down while Mona read and idly scratched the cat.

Chapter 3

Over The Edge

LA Guns

Joel sank gratefully into the tropical waters of the hot tub and closed his eyes.

Damn, it is unbelievably cold out here. The water feels great, though. Not exactly the peaceful night alone I was expecting. At least with Mona inside, I can spread out in the hot tub. I remember the last time I was in this hot tub and Cheri pulled off her—nope. Not going to think of my wife. Ex-wife. I wonder if she was already pregnant then. Was she trying to trick me into thinking the kid was mine?

He shook his head and reached for the whiskey bottle. The mouth of the bottle rested on his lips when he stopped.

Is this what I've come to? Getting shitfaced in a hot tub to drown my sorrows? Fuck. What if I get drunk, pass out, and drown for real? Would Mona bother to try to take me to a hospital if she found me face down in the hot tub? Would she care? She might dump my body in a ravine. Maybe I don't need a drink after all.

Joel carefully capped the bottle and set it down. "My mind can't stop going to dark places," he mumbled to his hooch.

The open mouth of the whiskey bottle didn't respond.

"And now I'm talking to a bottle of booze. Not exactly part of my five-year plan."

Cheri getting pregnant was in our plan, just not yet, and obviously not with her boss. Well, getting knocked up by Marc wasn't part of my plan, but apparently it became part of hers. Now I'm divorced, and he left his wife, and the two of them are happy—or not. She didn't look particularly thrilled when I signed the divorce papers. Oh well. Not my problem anymore.

Now, I need to start over, find a place to live, and somehow tell my parents what a colossal fuck-up their son is. I suppose I'll have to tell Tiffany, too. Preferably before she hears about it from Mona.

What am I going to do about Mona? She's absolutely right. It was a dick move to ghost her. Even more so after we lost our virginities together. I'm not entirely sure how to explain it all. I guess I could start with the truth.

Wait a second. Why do I even care? I haven't seen her since I graduated high school.

Joel spent the next half hour trying to find some kind of zen, but his mind returned again and again to the depressing litany of his thoughts. Finally heaving an exasperated sigh, he clambered out of the tub and returned to the cabin.

His uninvited orc guest looked up from her book as he walked in. "Huh. Good call on the robe. Definitely better than running naked to and from the hot tub."

"Yeah. There are more in the linen closet. Cheri's robes might not fit you."

Mona cocked an eyebrow at him. She growled, "Are you trying to say something?"

He stammered a response, "No, I...it's just...she was...is...shorter than you. And not as muscly. You know. Right?"

I sound like a complete moron. Wonderful.

"Uh-huh." Mona didn't sound convinced. "Whatever. If I need to, I'll wear one of your robes." She stopped scratching Bitsy long enough to point. "Are you planning on dripping on the floor all night?"

He looked down at the small puddle around his feet. "No, I..."

"I don't need a detailed explanation. It's your cabin. Do what you want." Mona returned to reading with a dismissive sniff.

He felt heat in his cheeks as he marched over to the linen closet and grabbed a towel. After drying his legs, he wiped up the puddle and hung the towel up in the small bathroom along with his swim trunks. Wrapping his robe tightly around himself, Joel tiptoed over to his luggage and rummaged around for something to wear. Grabbing clothes, he hustled back to the bathroom to put them on. Emerging thereafter, he said, "I'm about to make dinner. Do you want anything?"

If we're going to be stuck here together, I should try to be friendly and hope the gesture lightens the mood a bit. We'll be miserable if we're snapping at each other all the time.

"I don't know. What are you making?"

"Mac and cheese."

"*Ooh,* a master chef at work," Mona snarked from her chair.

"Hey, don't knock mac and cheese. Yes it's simple and from a box, which I admit is part of the draw after a long drive, but there's plenty of creative ways to liven it up."

She snorted, but the hard edge on her voice was softer when she said, "I'm hungry, so mac sounds good right now. I made some chili earlier if you want some."

"What kind of chili?"

Her eyes rolled back in her head. "You're offering me boxed macaroni and somehow my homemade chili isn't good enough?"

"I didn't—"

"*Whatever.* Beef and pinto beans."

"Your chili sounds amazing, and I can't wait to try some," he said with genuine enthusiasm.

"Much better."

Grateful to be past the awkward exchange, Joel started a pot of water boiling on the stovetop. He fussed about in the kitchenette to avoid further conversation with Mona. A glance over his shoulder revealed the orc and his cat relaxed in the chair.

Great. First my wife left me, and now my cat looks like she's getting cozy with someone else. I'm going to die alone.

He hauled the mac and chili over to the little table. "What do you want to drink?"

"I've already had a couple beers today, so I'll take water, please."

"Can I have one of your beers?"

Mona smirked. "Whiskey not good enough for you?"

"Hard liquor seemed like a fantastic idea at the store, but now it feels like a bit much."

She inclined her head ever so slightly. "Sure, have a beer."

They filled their plates and ate in silence while Bitsy twisted between their legs. Eventually, Joel couldn't take the hush anymore. "Your chili is excellent."

Mona grinned. "Your mac is boxed."

"Funny," he deadpanned. "Seriously though, I love a good chili, and everyone makes theirs differently. I didn't mean to insult you earlier."

Her look said she wasn't convinced. "What do you put in your chili?"

"Like you, beef and black beans. Also corn." She made a disgusted face when he said corn. "Also, I use green hatch chili powder from New Mexico."

"I'm not sold on the corn idea. At home, I use my own ancho and serrano blend, also from New Mexico."

"Nice." He stopped himself before he said anything else, not wanting to risk saying something stupid.

They ate for a while in an uncomfortable silence.

She stared at him as she chewed. Pointing her fork at him, she asked softly, "Do you want to talk about it?"

"It? You mean my divorce? The shitshow of my life?"

"Yeah."

"I don't know. Do you actually want to hear this?"

"No. Not really. I don't give a shit about your problems, but what else are we going to talk about tonight?"

Joel scoffed. "Not exactly a ringing endorsement. Plus, we could always talk about your shitshow of a life instead."

"*My* shitshow of a life?"

He pointed his fork at her. "You drove up to a mountain cabin—*on a motorcycle*—right before a blizzard."

"I will let you know that your sister told me it wasn't going to snow. Also, my life is not a shitshow."

"*Oh?*"

"It's a dumpster fire."

Joel guffawed. "Which is worse?"

"I have no idea."

"Me, either." He lowered his fork and looked over his hand at Mona's amethyst irises and the barest hint of a smile on her emerald lips. "Thank you for the offer. If I'm being honest, I'd rather not talk about my problems tonight. Or yours."

I'd rather talk about her eyes. Or her mouth. I forgot how pretty she is. Not just pretty...beautiful. Tiffany was an annoying little sister, but I never minded when she brought Mona around. The two of them teased me and bugged me, but Mona always had a magnetic something about her. Fierce. Smart. Wickedly funny.

"Hey, dumbass." Mona's voice cracked like a whip, snapping him out of his reverie.

"Wuh?"

"You said you didn't want to talk about our issues tonight and then you completely switched off. Are you tired or something?"

"Yeah. Totally exhausted. It's a long ass drive from Phoenix, especially in winter."

"True. Did you go through Nevada or California?"

"Nevada. Shorter and less mountains, although less interstate."

"Did you stop in Vegas for hookers and gambling?"

"Prostitution isn't legal in Vegas."

"And yet they are there," Mona retorted.

Joel's head was buzzing from the battery of questions. Taking a breath, he attempted to settle himself down. "True, but no, I did *not* stop in Vegas for either gambling or hookers. I had Bitsy with me and she kept me on the straight and narrow path."

Mona ducked down to scratch the cat. "You're a good girl, keeping your human away from a wastrel's life of excess. Yes, you are. Do you like it when I run my fingers under your little chin? Ohh, there's a purr. You must like it. You have very soft fur, Bitsy."

Thankful for the respite from Mona's inquisitive barrage, Joel ate his mac and chili in silence. His hopes for her continued distraction were dashed when her head popped up. "How long have you had Bitsy?"

"We...I got her about four years ago. Cheri said she wanted a pet, so we adopted Bitsy. Turns out, Bitsy liked me a lot more than she liked Cheri."

"Well, I'd say there's no accounting for taste, but she clearly likes me more than you." Mona grinned at him, toothy and teasing, before dipping her head below the table again. "Yes, you like me better, don't you? I might have to adopt you."

"*Hey.* No fair stealing my cat."

"I'm not stealing anyone. Bitsy is a smart girl," Mona scolded him. "Modern girls like us can make our own choices."

"She's just excited to see someone new."

Joel's heart skipped a beat as Mona's eyes rose above the lip of the table, dancing like glimmering pomegranate seeds.

"Yeah, someone new who isn't stupid enough to drive her around in a blizzard. Us smart girls need to stick together, Bitsy. We don't need any moron men messing up our lives."

"I didn't—" Her scowl froze the words in his throat. Ratcheting down his tone to a gentle level, Joel responded, "I've taken very good care of Bitsy all of her life. She's been my best friend, which sounds pathetic once I hear it out loud, but it's true."

Mona cooed at the feline. "Aw, you are a good girl."

They finished their meal in silence, and Joel collected the dishes to wash them. Meanwhile, Mona and Bitsy settled down on the chair again, one of them reading and the other napping. He walked over once he was done and cleared his throat.

"Yes?" Limpid lilac pools glittered at him from under a cocked auburn eyebrow. Joel's train of thought derailed again, so Mona continued speaking. "You're probably wondering about sleeping arrangements."

"Right. Exactly. This is my place, so I figured I'd take the bed, and I'll get out the air mattress for you."

Mona's eyes narrowed into slits and her lips pulled back, revealing the miniature tusks on her lower jaw. Instincts which kept his long-distant ancestors alive when saber-toothed tigers stalked the night kicked into high gear.

"Or...you could have the bed, and I'll take the air mattress. You're right. Much better plan. I'll just blow up the mattress."

He hustled over to the bench slash storage box underneath the western window. Pulling out the air mattress box, he immediately noted the trail of detritus filtering out of a hole. Peering inside, he could immediately see the damage. He waved the box in the air as he spun around to face Mona.

"We have a problem. It appears a mouse ate into the air mattress. Not all of it, of course."

"Ew."

"No problem." Joel waved his free hand dismissively. "I'll just sleep in a chair. Or on the floor. It'll be fine."

"Sounds good. I'm going to read for a bit more, if you don't mind." She stroked Bitsy's back absently as she spoke, eliciting a rumbly purr from the contented feline.

He shifted his weight from one foot to the other and back, running a hand through his hair. Licking his lips, he ventured, "I didn't bring any books. Could I borrow one of yours?"

"How do you not have a stash of books up here? What did you and what's-her-face do to pass the time?" Her eyebrows knitted into a frown. "Never mind. I can guess."

"It's not what you think." He could see an auburn eyebrow arch. "Well, it *is* what you think, but we also read books and stuff."

"And stuff." She smirked.

Joel sniffed. "*Yes...*like card games or board games."

Her eyebrow arched a bit higher and those lavender eyes grew a bit brighter before she returned her focus to her book and Bitsy. "Yeah. Fine," she muttered.

Huh. It almost appeared as if she was interested in the idea of games. Maybe I'm imagining things. I hope not. Might as well see what she has to read.

"Where are your books? Is there one in particular I should read? Or not read?"

"Not really, unless you're a slow reader. My books are in my backpack up in the loft," she said dismissively, not even bothering to look up from her book and cat scratching.

"Thanks, Mona. I appreciate it."

Joel walked up the spiral staircase into the upper portion of the cabin. He ignored the unkempt bed and located the large, weather-proof rucksack leaning against the small dresser. Opening the bag, he reached inside. His hand closed around a hard, curved metal rod, which he pulled out of the pack.

"*Holy fuck, don't go in my bag,*" Mona shouted from below, accompanied by an agitated howl from Bitsy.

"Too late." Joel stared at the curved steel in his palm, unsure of what to make of it. Heavy feet pounded up the stairs behind him. He could feel Mona's presence behind his shoulder blades and briefly pondered if his life was about to come to a very abrupt end.

"I told you not to go in my bag," she hissed.

He felt the hairs on the back of his neck stiffen.

Do I turn around and face her, or stay as I am? I'm honestly unsure which choice is worse. Maybe facing her would be better? Which ravine will she dump my body in?

"In my defense, you *did* tell me I could borrow a book and they were in your backpack," he said as evenly as possible. Completing his slow turn, he could see her snarling expression. Beyond the clenched teeth, he noted how her cheeks, usually the color of a green olive, were closer to the hue of cooked spinach.

Both sets of eyes drifted down to the gleaming metal object in his hand. A quick upward flick of his eyes revealed her pointed ears also turning spinach dark.

Her voice rasped like a sharp steel blade sliding from a leather sheath. "Put. It. Down."

Joel searched for a convenient spot to unload the silvery rod from his care. He didn't dare drop it, but wasn't sure how long her patience would last while he came to a decision. His amygdala, aware of the imminent danger, overrode his dithering logic center and directed him to place the weighty object on the dresser behind him.

"I'm very sorry, Mona. I have—" His voice trailed off when clarity struck. Now he realized what he had been holding. Joel's brain was suddenly strapped to a metaphorical rocket blasting him from the reality of having held Mona's dildo to the swirling bright orbital casino of speculation about where the steel rod had been and what pleasures it must have evoked.

"Fucking hell, Joel."

"I'm terribly sorry. I didn't know what was in your bag."

Her shoulders slumped. "It's my fault for being distracted by a purring cat. I should have remembered what else I brought beyond books."

"You did come up here to relax, and I'm sure—"

"*Joel*," she interrupted. "Don't you dare finish your thought."

"Right." He gulped. In the lightest and breeziest tone he could summon, Joel suggested, "Why don't I go downstairs while you pick out a book for me. Any book is okay. Anything at all. I'm not picky."

"You're babbling."

"Yes, I definitely am. I'm also going now." He hustled for the stairs, feeling her glare between his shoulder blades the whole way.

Joel tucked himself into a cozy chair near the wood stove and waited for Mona to come downstairs. She eventually did, handing him a book.

"Romance?"

"I swear, if you give me shit about my books—"

"*No.* No. It's fine."

"What? You think orcs don't have complex feelings?" He could hear the anger building in her tone.

"Of course not."

"Oh, you think romance is stupid and thus perfect for orcs?"

"No. It's just..."

"*Yes?*" Mona's eyes were the purple color of the underbelly of a thunderhead about to unleash lightning and misery, and her fangs were fully on display.

"I remember you reading mostly mysteries back when we were growing up."

"Oh." The thunderclouds dissipated a bit. "I still enjoy a good mystery. Honestly, give me a good mystery mixed with romance, and I'm hooked."

"Hey, Mona." He beheld her standing before him, arms crossed defensively over her chest. His pulse quickened as he tried not to stare.

"What?" She snapped, but her cheeks flushed subtly.

"I've never thought less of you because you're an orc. You've been an incredible, supportive friend to Tiffany all these years. She's needed you in her life to keep her grounded. Thank you for looking after my baby sister. You're smart, capable, and overall amazing."

Mona huffed, then grunted, "Thanks," before she wheeled around. She picked up her book and flopped down in her chair.

What did I say? I thought I was being nice. Should I have added the part about how I compare every woman I've ever dated to her, and none of them ever measured up, including my ex-wife? No. It's probably best I didn't.

Chapter 4

Bad Idea, Right?

Olivia Rodrigo

The scraping of chair legs on the wood floor brought Mona out of deep sleep, but it was the subsequent crash and cursing which jolted her awake. She stared at the ceiling in the darkness, listening to Joel flail about downstairs. Her ears picked up every tiny groan and whimper as he tried to find a comfortable position.

He's obviously trying not to make a racket, but he's clearly not used to sleeping around the sensitive ears of orcs. Joel already fell out of the chair, and he is never going to find a comfortable position on a hardwood floor. I'm either going to have to listen to him toss and turn all night or share the bed with him. Ugh. I don't want to share a bed with him. Of course, if I don't, then neither of us will get any sleep. We'll both be tired and snappy all day tomorrow. Plus, he'll absolutely be an idiot man about the aches and pains from trying to sleep on the floor, meaning he'll somehow simultaneously refuse to talk about how much he hurts while also being a gigantic baby about the agonizing pain he's suffering.

"Joel?" she called out softly, half hoping he wouldn't hear her over his own noises.

"Huh?"

Mona sighed, partially disappointed. "Get up here. We'll share the bed."

"I'm okay."

Men. Doesn't matter the species. They're all idiots.

"No. You're not. I can hear your muscles cramping from here."

"How?"

"I'm an orc, you dumbass. These bigass ears aren't just for deco-ration."

"I didn't know. I'll be quieter."

Breathe, Mona. Just breathe. He can't help himself.

"Joel, you nitwit. Get your ass up here now, because no one is going to be happy if I have to come down there and haul you up the fucking stairs. I think we both know I'm more than capable of doing just that."

"Okay," he muttered.

Goddess, guide me on the path of peace and serenity so I may not strangle this human. I don't even need to see his face to know he's pouting. I can hear it in his voice.

She heard him trudge up the stairs like a scolded child. As his face came into view, she confirmed his sullen visage.

"Stop sulking, Joel."

"I'm—how did you know?"

"Have you not paid any attention? My hearing is superior to humans, and I see better in the darkness, too."

"I'm just not used to being around orcs much."

"Not good enough for you?"

"Cheri always felt nervous around…"

Even he knows how silly his excuse sounds.

"I don't bite, but if you snore or touch me, then you're going to regret it."

He nodded somberly. "Noted."

Mona rolled over and closed her eyes. She felt the mattress dip as Joel slid under the covers. After a brief spate of jostling for the blankets, they each settled down.

She woke up some time later feeling warm and sweaty. The loft was still dark as she opened her eyes. The reality of her situation quickly ripped away the fog of sleep. She was pressed into Joel's back, with one arm draped across his soft midsection. Behind her knees was a heavy, warm mass.

Shit. I'm spooning him. Maybe he's not awake. I hope he's not awake.

"Mona?" he asked, voice quivering slightly.

Fuck.

"Yes, Joel?"

"I feel like now would be a good time to clarify something. When you mentioned me regretting it if I touched you in the night, did your warning also pertain to you touching me?"

"As in, am I going to beat your ass to a bloody pulp because I touched you?" She sighed and sent a silent plea for strength to the Goddess. "No, but I'm certainly asking myself why I didn't let you suffer on the floor, though."

"Not going to lie, I'm wondering the same thing; however, my back appreciates your kindness and generosity."

"Your back is welcome. Also, I can't move my legs."

"Bitsy likes to curl up behind my knees in the middle of the night."

"Aw, she's—"

Mona was about to add the word *adorable*, but her speech died as she moved her arm. She intended to remove her arm from around Joel and then reach behind herself to pet the cat, but the process was immediately interrupted by contact with a hard cylindrical object.

"*Ew.* Are you hard?"

He protested vociferously. "It's not my fault. This is a normal human condition."

"Gross. Get out, get out, *get out!*" She pushed him toward the edge of the bed. Bitsy squeaked behind her, and the big cat clambered up onto her legs.

"Okay, okay. I'm going away." Joel threw off the covers and stood up, a decision they both quickly regretted.

Mona saw the prominent tent in the front of Joel's shorts before he hunched over and covered himself with his hands. She choked out a cry and buried her head under the blankets.

"Goddess, Joel. What is *wrong* with you?" she exclaimed.

"I'm sorry. I can't help it."

She peeked out from under the covers. "Just go the hell away and take your little problem downstairs."

His face a brilliant scarlet, Joel mumbled, "Okay." He whirled and shuffled down the spiral staircase.

Joel's problem wasn't very little at all. I haven't seen his dick in fifteen years, but I recall it was a nice one. Stop thinking about his schlong, Mona. The sex was terrible and then he dumped you. Didn't even dump you. Ghosted you. Of course, the sex was awful—we were teenagers who didn't know what the hell we were doing. I'm much better at sex now. He might not be, especially if his wife left him. Maybe he's still incompetent in the sack. Great. I'm still thinking about his wang. I was already horny before I came up here, and I never got around to taking care of business before Joel arrived. Now I've got dick on the brain. Fuck. Get your shit together, girl.

Mona rolled out of bed and peeled off her tank top. Hanging up the damp garment, she slipped on a new tank top before descending from the loft. Joel was puttering in the kitchenette, trying to avoid stepping on a frantic Bitsy. "Do you need me to distract her?"

"Yes," he breathed out a grateful sigh. "She is always desperate for food. You'd think I've never fed her."

Scooping up the hefty cat, Mona buried her nose in the cat's soft fur. "Clearly, you do feed her. Otherwise she wouldn't be such a big girl. There's nothing wrong with being a big girl. You are just the right size for you. Aren't you, Bitsy?"

Peering over the feline at Joel, Mona asked, "Why did you name her Bitsy anyway?"

He shrugged. "You know how sometimes huge guys are nick-named Tiny?"

"Seriously?" She shook her head and rolled her eyes. "Bitsy, I am so sorry you were named by an imbecile. You probably have a much more dignified name in your own head. Something like Itsabella, Great Huntress of the Fluffy Paws."

Joel snorted. "*What?*"

"It's a better name than Bitsy," she huffed. Mona stuck her nose in the air haughtily. "I shall call her Itsabella from now on."

"You're going to confuse her."

"No, I won't. Right, Itsabella? You're a smart girl, and us smart girls need to stick together. Especially around dumb boys." Mona grinned into Itsabella's fur, thoroughly enjoying the exasperated expression on Joel's face.

I shouldn't enjoy teasing someone, but he deserves every dose of shit I can pile onto him. At least his dong isn't tenting his shorts anymore. For a guy who isn't in great shape, he does have a particularly nice ass. Nice ass? What the hell is wrong with you, Mona? It's been a while, but there's no excuse for checking out his butt. Any other butt on the entire planet is fine to look at. Just not his.

"Mona? Hey, Mona." Joel waved a hand at her.

"Huh?"

"You can put—" He sighed with an exaggerated heave of his shoulders. "—Itsabella down now. Her breakfast is ready."

She didn't bother to hide her triumphantly toothy grin as she squatted to release the feline. Itsabella rumbled over to her bowl and devoured her breakfast.

"Wow. I haven't seen anyone attack their food with such gusto. And I grew up with two brothers who played football."

"How are Rick and Russell?"

"Fine, I guess." She smiled despite herself when she realized he remembered her siblings' names." Rick is still playing football. He plays for San Antonio in the Orc League. Russell went into the army. He's stationed in North Carolina."

"Your folks must miss them."

Mona grunted. "Not really. Once it became clear Rick and Russell were going to be out East for good, they moved about seven years ago to be closer to their boys."

She studied the confused expression on his face.

"Trying to figure out the right words to say?"

He grimaced. "Yeah. Pretty much."

She infused her voice with as much snark as she could to bury the pain. "There's no good way to say 'Wow, it sucks to be undervalued because of your gender' to someone you also ditched at the first opportunity."

"Mona, I'm sorry for how I treated you back then. It wasn't right."

"Whatever." She spun on her heel and strode over to the wood stove. Adding wood to the stove and adjusting the airflow to increase heat was not an adequate distraction from the anger, loneliness, abandonment, and latent humiliation she felt.

It's bad enough to be treated as filth by humans and elves because I'm an orc, but to be treated as filth by my own family because I'm a woman is even worse. A significant portion of humanity treats human women just as badly as orcs treat their women, but somehow it's accept-able because they're human? I fucking hate hypocrites. Especially Joel. What was up with him last night? Telling me how much he admires me, as if I'll somehow forgive him for how he treated me all those years ago? What an asshole.

Her nose twitched.

"Do I smell bacon?"

"Yes," he called out. "I should have asked, Do you want some?"

"Are elves assholes?"

Joel snickered. "No. Not at all. In my experience, they're univer-sally delightful. In fact, they're almost as nice as this bacon I'll have to eat all by myself."

Mona growled, then sighed. *It's no fun wasting a good growl be-cause humans can't hear for shit.*

To Joel, she said, "You know what I meant."

"Of course I do. I assume you still like egg and cheese as well?"

"Yes. Are you making me a breakfast sandwich?"

His back was turned, but she could hear the grin in his voice. "Yep. Sorry it's on toast. The store didn't have any bagels. Well, they had bagels, but they didn't have *good* bagels. I like mine at least somewhat fresh and not pumped full of preservatives."

"Me too." She stifled a grunt. Joel was being exceptionally pleas-ant and she didn't like it, yet couldn't object, either. *It's hard to be pissed at him when he's making me my favorite breakfast sandwich. I remember sleepovers with Tiffany when we were kids and Joel would make us breakfast. His parents would try so hard to ignore the little orc in their house.* Trying to keep the grumpiness out of her voice, she said, "Thank you. Can I help?"

"Yeah. Can you grab a couple small plates and bring them over? Also, there's pineapple juice in the fridge."

"Pineapple?"

"What?" Joel twisted his head around to peer over his shoulder. "Please tell me you don't have any objections, because pineapple is the fucking best."

Mona set two plates next to Joel. "I don't think I've ever had pineapple juice, but I do love fresh pineapple."

He moaned. "Me too. It's like candy, but healthy."

"Truth. Do you need anything else?"

"Nope. I'll be done in a minute."

She sat down and waited briefly at the table before he brought over the two plates. Her stomach rumbled as he set her plate down.

"Sorry. It's whole wheat toast. Or multigrain. I don't know. Something healthy. I'm trying to eat better."

The corners of Mona's mouth twitched upward. "Bacon probably doesn't help."

"Baby steps."

"Uh-huh," she grunted dubiously as she picked up her sandwich. Taking a bite, she reveled in the taste. "Did you add garlic?"

"Of course. I recall you always liked your eggs scrambled in butter with salt, pepper, and a touch of garlic powder."

"Are you kidding me? You still remember how I liked my eggs from when I was a kid?"

Joel's eyebrows arched. "Anytime you came over, Mom and Dad had me fix breakfast for you and Tiff." He leaned back in his chair. "I remember one weekend my folks went away. You came over to spend the night, and you wanted egg sandwiches and home fries for dinner *and* for breakfast the next day."

The sandwich suddenly tasted like ash in her mouth. "I remember. You asked me out that weekend," she snarled. "Two weeks later you fucked me and dumped me."

"Oh shit, Mona. I'm sorry."

"You keep apologizing, Joel, but I don't believe you." She leapt up from the table and bolted upstairs, leaving her half-eaten sandwich and a slack-jawed Joel behind. Tumbling into the bed, she pulled the blankets over her head and let the tears flow.

Fucking bastard. I almost forgot why I hated him and then it all came crashing back. For a minute, things between us were sweet and pleasant. Never forget, Mona. Never forget.

She cried herself to sleep eventually, Itsabella pressed up against her.

Chapter 5

Fifteen

Taylor Swift

I'm such a fucking idiot. For a brief instant we were having a cordial conversation, and then I had to bring up old memories. I wish I knew what to do. She doesn't seem to care when I tell her I'm sorry. Somehow, I need to figure out a way to communicate my feelings to Mona. I can't believe how lucky I am to have her here at my cabin. Being snowed in gives me the second chance I've always wanted, provided I don't blow it. You know, like I'm currently doing.

In the moments when the wind outside died down, he could hear Mona crying. The sense of relief he felt when the wind drowned out her weeping both embarrassed and revolted him. He watched Bitsy ascend to the loft, and he silently wished her well.

Bitsy has an incredible sense for when someone needs comfort. A warm purring cat snuggling next to you doesn't fix every problem, but it certainly helps. I could use some comforting from my own internal issues, but clearly Mona needs Bitsy more. In the meantime, I need to figure out how to not be a bag of dicks. The biggest step has to be honesty, although I'm not certain the truth will help. Sincerity is a risk I'm going to have to take. The question is, when is the right moment?

Thinking of the right moment—I should have known something was wrong with Cheri when she started pushing Bitsy away. My cat is clearly more emotionally aware than I am.

Joel tried unsuccessfully to read for over an hour, but his mind was too absorbed by his swirling thoughts. He finally gave up. Hearing Mona's soft snores from the loft, he threw out her half-eaten breakfast and changed into his swim trunks. Cursing the cold, he dashed for the hot tub and yanked off the cover. Sinking blissfully into the warm water, he surveyed mountain woods around him.

"We're definitely going to be here for a few days," he muttered to himself. Closing his eyes, he let the hot tub try to work its relaxing magic on his body and troubled mind. While his body felt better, his brain rocketed out of control. Recriminations about his failed marriage blended with guilt and shame surrounding his relationships with his family and Mona. The toxic stew inside his psyche made his temples throb and pound like an all-night rave.

Unable to find peace, Joel heaved a sigh and pulled himself out of the water. Icy daggers pricked his skin as he covered the hot tub and sprinted for the cabin door. Inside, he toweled himself dry and warmed his chilled skin in front of the wood stove. After pulling on clothes and boots, he grabbed the snow shovel from the small closet and tromped out the front door.

He shoveled a path from the front door to the woodpile and Mona's motorcycle, then extended the cleared section all the way to his car. The snow was almost halfway covering his tires and more was still falling, although at a gentler pace than the previous day. Shoveling snow was the kind of mind-numbing physical activity he needed to finally quell the turbulence in his head. Soaked with sweat despite the chill, he finished clearing around his car before retracing his pathway to the cabin.

His stomach growled as he pulled off his snow-encrusted boots. Once he changed into sweatpants and a t-shirt, he trotted across the cabin to make himself a sandwich. After devouring one sandwich, he fixed two more. Rummaging through the cabinets, he found a tray and stacked two plates of sandwiches, two glasses of water, and a pair of beers on the tray. Gingerly carrying the tray up the spiral staircase, he sat down on the bed.

"Go away," Mona grunted into the pillow.

"I brought you lunch."

"Fuck off."

"Black pepper turkey and cheddar sandwich and either water or beer." He paused before adding, "Or both."

The lumpy mass under the blankets stirred. "Cold sandwich or hot?"

"It's cold, but I can toast it up for you, if you'd like."

"Yes, please." The volume of her voice dropped to barely audible. "Thanks, Joel."

"You're welcome. I'll be back in a couple minutes. In the meantime, I'll put the tray on the dresser so the drinks don't spill."

Taking the two plates, he descended the stairs and set the plates on the counter before he fished out a frying pan and olive oil. He returned upstairs shortly thereafter with grilled turkey and cheese sandwiches.

Mona was sitting up in the bed, her face streaked with the detritus of tears. She kept her head down as she pawed at her cheeks. "Don't look at me," she whined.

He placed a plate on the bed between them before sitting down, carefully facing away from her. "I'm not looking, I promise," he responded in a calm and even voice. "Can we talk about it?"

"Talk about what?"

He heard the edge of a sniffle in her voice. Not wanting to send her into tears again, he ventured into self-deprecation. "We could talk about how I'm a colossal asshole."

"You're not an asshole, Joel. Assholes have a useful function."

He winced but plunged onward. "Ouch. I deserve it though."

She munched on her sandwich behind him, letting him stew in the silence before asking, "Fine, since you can't take a hint and aren't leaving, I'll bite. Why, Joel? Why did you ditch me?"

"It's complicated."

"Last I checked, we're not going anywhere, are we?"

"No. We're snowed in." Joel's shoulders collapsed and his back hunched as he prepared to tell the truth. "The day after we had our date—"

"And sex."

"Right. The next day, Tiff and I were in the kitchen and she was teasing me about the two of us and whether we did the deed, and my parents overheard. It wasn't Tiffany's fault. She was just being an annoying little sister and also protective of her best friend. Anyway, my parents freaked out."

"Your parents are racist shitbags," Mona growled, the sound rumbling in her throat.

Joel nodded. "I know. I knew it back then, too, but I didn't feel the truth of it when I was a teenager like I do now."

She grunted and he imagined her sitting on the bed with her arms folded.

"Mona, can I turn around?"

"Hang on."

He felt the blankets move and heard rustling.

"Fine. You can turn around."

Joel maneuvered himself to partially face Mona. His right leg hung off the bed while his left was tucked up. Spotting a cozy spot to nest, Bitsy strutted over and plunked down in the crook behind his left knee, although she was so big she spilled over his leg.

"My parents waited until Tiff was gone, then they ambushed me. They threatened to kick me out of the house and not give me money for college unless I swore to never see you or speak to you again."

Her eyes burned with amaranthine fire. Mona snapped, "And you rolled over like a fucking poodle and did what they asked?"

"I argued with them, of course. I love you, and I tried to reason with them."

"You still caved."

"Mona, I was seventeen years old. They were threatening to kick me out, and I remember being so scared. I didn't know what else to do. If I could go back and do it over, I'd like to think I would have taken my chances."

"Why didn't you tell me?"

He searched desperately for an answer. There were plenty of answers to be had, and each one was worse than the one before. Instead he fell into silence, gawping like a landed trout.

"Because you're a fucking coward," she hissed.

"I'm sorry. I was seventeen."

"Yeah, and I was fifteen, you brainless jizzrag." Rage was clearly building in Mona's body language. Her eartips quivered, the muscles on her arms corded, and the tips of her fangs protruded above her lower lip. "You told me you loved me, and I gave you *everything* and then you left me hanging without a word because you were too fucking scared of your parents to stand up for the person you supposedly loved. *Fuck you, Joel.* Do you have any idea what you did to me?"

He hung his head in shame, any words of remorse strangled in his collapsing throat.

"I loved you back, and then all I'm left to feel is rejected and worthless. You know, like an *orc.*"

Joel managed to summon a brief reply. "It was never about you being an orc."

"It sure as hell was for your parents, and because you went along with them, it was for you, too."

"I never cared about your species or your green skin. It was always about who you were as a person."

"*Fuck off.*"

They sat there in an awkward silence, finally broken when Mona asked in a small voice, "Did Tiffany know?"

"No. I never told her, and I'm pretty sure my parents didn't, either."

"Good," Mona growled.

"If it makes you feel better, Tiff barely spoke to me for the rest of my senior year. She thought I was being a huge asshole—"

Mona snorted. "Because you are one."

He shook off her insult and continued on. "To this day, Tiff still doesn't talk with me much, and she *hated* Cheri. She's *always* been on your side, Mona. It's kind of funny. Right before my wedding, Tiff told me I was marrying the wrong woman."

"Aw. My girl has my back."

"Just like you have hers. You always have."

Mona's eyes narrowed.

Okay, she's still not accepting compliments from me.

"You know what makes this whole shitshow even worse?" She didn't wait for an answer, barrelling forward. "You dumped me for college money from your parents, and then you didn't even finish college. So you sacrificed our relationship for nothing."

"I'm sorry—"

"Why, Joel? If college was more important than me, then what was more important than college?"

No matter what, she's going to hate my answer, so I might as well be completely honest.

"My whole life, my parents drilled into me how important it was for me to go to college to get a good job. Then I got there and nothing worked for me. Okay…some things clicked. Unfortunately, they don't give degrees in beer pong."

Mona's face twisted into an expression of disgust.

"I switched majors on a monthly basis, but nothing was right. My sophomore year, I became something of the go-to handyman on Greek Row. I dropped out soon after and apprenticed as an electrician."

"You're an electrician?"

"Yeah. Honestly, it's a great job. Decent hours, good pay. I get to work with my hands and solve problems. What? Not good enough for you?"

Mona sneered at him. "Electrician is about the best job an orc can hope for. Usually, we only get the shittiest jobs imaginable. My last job was beating the shit out of anyone who grabbed a stripper's ass on stage. I've cleaned buildings and houses. Houses were the worst, because the homeowners would watch over you constantly because they expected you to rob them the moment they looked away. Whatever the worst jobs you can think of are, I've worked them or I know an orc who has."

He opened his mouth to speak and quickly shut it when he recognized her scowl.

"Don't you dare tell me how sorry you are. I don't want your worthless pity. What I want is fucking justice." Eyes shining with ultraviolet fire drilled into his. "You know what else I want? For you to have finished college. I don't give a shit if you would have been miserable. Honestly, your misery would have been a bonus for me."

Shocked, Joel's gaze rose to meet Mona's. "Why?"

"Because you *chose* the life you wanted. I don't get those choices because I was born an orc. I was born in this country by happenstance. Any human or elf born in this country is automatically a citizen. But not me. Not any other orc or half-orc, either." Her fangs flashed in the dim sunlight as the volume of her voice increased as she went on. "We're considered subhuman, and because of it, we're denied opportunities based on our birth. The worst part is, y'all did the same shit to humans of non-European ancestry for centuries *and learned absofuckinglutely nothing from it,*" she finished in a shout.

He stared at the sheets. "I understand."

"Do you?"

Joel forced his gaze up to meet hers. "No. Not fully. It's an experience I'll never have, but I get why you're angry and frustrated. You should be; because it's wrong."

Mona sneered at him. "Wrong is such a cowardly word. Try evil, cruel, and immoral. You know, everything supposedly baked into the DNA of orcs."

Unable to find words, he hung his head in shame.

"Joel?" Her voice was softer now, brittle.

"Yeah?"

"Can you leave me alone for a bit?"

"Of course." He lifted Bitsy off his leg and stood. She crawled over to Mona and settled in with her new friend. He turned to leave.

As he set foot on the top step, Mona's voice brought him to an abrupt halt.

"Joel?"

"Yes, Mona?"

"Thanks for lunch and for talking."

"You're welcome."

61

Chapter 6

I Can Do It With A Broken Heart

Taylor Swift

"I love you, and I tried to reason with them." The words echoed in Mona's skull.

Not loved. Love, as in present tense. Was it just a slip of the tongue? What if he was speaking too fast and he said it wrong? Or does Joel claim to love me still, fifteen years later? Why didn't he correct himself? Did he even notice? I can't stop thinking about one stupid word. Not a stupid word, just a stupid human man. An over-entitled coward of a stupid human man.

She could hear him downstairs cleaning dishes and giving her the space she asked for. Twisting her body, Mona planted herself face down in a pillow. The cushion swallowed her frustrated groan.

Why did he have to come to this cabin of all places while I'm here? Couldn't he have gone to Vegas for his early mid-life crisis like a normal human? Oh right. The cat. He could have easily put Itsabella in a cat hotel and spent a debauched week of gambling, drinking, and whoring like a decent person. But no, he has to come here, and now we're snowed in together.

Mona pushed herself up and rolled onto her side so she could properly share the bed with Itsabella. The big fluffy feline bonked Mona's nose with the top of her head. A rumbling purr competed with the wind in Mona's ears. She found both sounds soothing in different ways.

You know what isn't soothing? Joel tunelessly singing Taylor Swift. He was not blessed with a great singing voice. He's trying, though, and it's kind of cute, albeit painful.

Mona sighed.

"Cute, albeit painful" is a good description of Joel and this entire situation. I don't want to think of Joel as cute, even if he is. Not quite as musclebound hot as he was in high school, especially with the sad comb-over, but still attractive in a different way now. Then again, we've all changed since high school.

Fuck. I'm not going to convince myself to give him a second chance. I don't want him in my life—not now, not ever. Stupid snow.

Downstairs, Joel unsuccessfully chased a high note.

How is his singing so bad?

She buried her head in Itsabella's furry flank. The rumbling purring couldn't drown out Joel's singing, but it helped. Running her fingers through soft fur brought a smile to her lips and a sigh from her throat. "I may not approve of your choice of humans, Itsabella, but I'm glad I met you. You're the sweetest cat."

Itsabella answered with a head bonk.

Mona curled herself around the big Maine Coon and snuggled close. They both susurrated happily.

What would I have done differently if I were Joel? Besides not being a fucking coward about not explaining what was going on, probably not much. My parents never told me I was good enough to do anything. Society at large wrote me off the moment I was born. I can barely comprehend the pressure of being told the key to success lay down one sacrosanct path and then having my access threatened. He should have talked to me. I'm still angry with him for ghosting me. At least now I finally know why.

There's a certain freedom in knowing it's not me, it was all him—and his parents.

Lying in bed listening to cat snores, blowing wind, and off-key singing was surprisingly relaxing. Mona lay on her side, contemplating the shifting patterns of brown, red, and white fur on Itsabella's chest as she breathed. Itsabella's eyes opened, and she gave Mona a look as if to say, "Why are you staring at me, orc? Shouldn't you take a nap as well?"

She whispered, "I already slept a lot today, little girl. We can't all be cats, you know."

Itsabella closed her eyes and fell asleep again.

"You're very lucky to be a cat. I'd like to sleep all day."

Mona quietly observed her feline bedmate, letting Itsabella's snoring guide her into a semi-meditative state. Her trance was broken by Joel's garbled voice and the sound of the back door opening and closing. Curious, she uncoiled herself, eliciting a sullen squeak from Itsabella. Padding downstairs, she found the main floor of the cabin empty. Peering outside, she saw Joel in the hot tub with one of her beers dangling from an outstretched hand.

Well...shit. I can spend all day in bed with a cat, feeling all kinds of fucked up, or I could be social with another biped for a bit, even if it's Joel. Of course, the lack of a bikini is an issue, but not an insurmountable one.

She climbed back upstairs and dove into her limited supply of clothes. After changing into an AC/DC t-shirt and skintight boy shorts, she walked to the stairs. She paused at the top.

This is a bad idea, right? In retrospect, risking a blizzard at an isolated mountain cabin was a bad idea even before Joel got here. What's a little more stupidity? Fuck it, it's fine.

Mona descended the stairs and pulled a beer from the fridge. Stepping outside, she was greeted by freezing air and Joel's off-key rendition of yet another Taylor Swift song. Sucking in a frigid breath, Mona added her contralto voice, singing along to the next line.

She snickered when he stopped singing, his head whipping around. The icy wind plucked at her skin, but she suppressed a shiver. In spite of the frigid atmosphere, she strutted slowly to the hot tub.

Screw the cold. I'm an orc. I can manage a little chill better than any human. Not only do I get to prove my strength, but I'm going to enjoy watching his expression as he realizes what he's been missing out on for all these years because of his cowardice.

Mona took a swig of her beer before climbing up and lifting one emerald leg over the side. She observed his eyes fixated on her taut, muscled flesh. His gaze traveled from calf to thigh to the forbidden realm in between as she lifted her other leg and swung it over, closing off his glimpse of paradise.

The heat from the water contrasting with her chilled skin almost broke her resolve, but she managed to bury a moan before it could escape her throat. She glided languorously into the water, her AC/DC t-shirt billowing as the lower hem caught a jet from the hot tub. An anticipatory gleam flared in Joel's eyes, but his hopes were dashed as she slid her shoulders under the water.

"Don't let me interrupt your singing, Joel. I'm sure Ms. Swift would be quite impressed."

"Really?" he asked with an irrepressible flicker of hope in his expression.

She snorted. "Impressed? *No.* Appalled? *Definitely.*"

He sighed, a mournful expression on his face. "I know I'm a bad singer. I guess I hoped I'd improved with practice somehow."

Now I feel a bit guilty for crushing his spirit.

"Maybe stick with something more in your range? Like industrial, or heavy metal."

Joel looked offended. "*Not cool.* There have been some absolutely amazing heavy metal singers."

"Like who?"

"Halford. Dickinson. Dio."

"You're shitting me," Mona responded with a snort.

He frowned. "Have you listened to them? I mean, *really* listened?"

"I'm sure I've probably heard something of theirs. Who are they?"

His eyes rolled back into his head. "I'll be right back." Joel handed her his beer and pulled himself out of the water. "*Holy shit,*" he squealed as the frigid air raised a bumper crop of goosebumps. He raced for the cabin and shut the door. He re-emerged a couple minutes later with his phone in hand. "*Fucking shit.* It's somehow even worse the second time."

Joel raced for the hot tub, barely managing to keep his phone dry as he sank into the tropical water with a blissful sigh.

"You're going to make me listen, aren't you?"

His frown conveyed a deep level of scorn. "Come on, Mona, you're wearing an AC/DC shirt. How do you know nothing about heavy metal?"

"Obviously, I know *something*. I like a bunch of AC/DC songs. You can't be a strip club bouncer as long as I have without hearing "You Shook Me All Night Long" a thousand times. Same with Def Leppard's "Pour Some Sugar On Me." I'm not completely ignorant, you know."

"At least you've heard some songs. I see kids these days with metal band shirts, and I wonder if they've ever heard an AC/DC or G'N'R song. Anyway, let me play you something."

"What is it?"

He gave her a look which practically begged for patience. "Just listen, okay?"

She nodded as a drum solo kicked off the song. Guitars ushered in an eerie aura which the singer used as a backdrop to a sprawling saga of sweating workers building a skyhigh tower for a wizard to reach the stars. When the wizard fails to fly and comes crashing to Earth, she felt the singer's dismay and confusion at the senseless waste of lives for a fool's hubris and his burning desire to return to his faraway home.

"Well? What do you think?" Joel asked with an eager jitteriness.

"Play it again."

"Again?"

Mona cocked an eyebrow. "Did I stutter?" Joel restarted the song, and Mona let herself submerge in the music. As it ended the second time, she said, "Okay, you've proved your point. That's pretty damn good. What's the song?"

"It's 'Stargazer' by *Rainbow* with Ronnie James Dio on vocals."

"This is nothing like what you listened to in high school."

Joel's shoulders rose briefly out of the water as he shrugged. "Well, you spend enough time running wires on worksites and you hear a very broad range of music. I'm not necessarily a fan of everything I heard, but I can appreciate most of it to some degree."

"Ooh, very multicultural of you."

"You mock me, but it's been an eye-opening experience overall. I've also learned to speak Spanish and *Urugrim*."

"*Dak shar bat grum kai?*"

"*Kin gom mat lir.*"

She cringed. "Ugh. Your accent is terrible."

"It's not my fault." Joel cleared his throat. "Speaking Orc makes me feel like I'm about to cough up a lung."

Mona chuckled. "You aren't wrong. If I'm being honest, your accent is better than most humans. You all usually sound like a life-long smoker with pneumonia."

"Wow..."

"Oh shut up, Joel. I know Orc is a tough language. Trust me, it sucks for me, too, and I grew up speaking it. Now play some more music. Also, how do you have any signal up here?"

He fumbled with his phone before playing something else for her. "I don't. I downloaded a playlist or two before I started my trip."

"Let me guess, you made a recently divorced mood playlist."

Joel's face, already pink from the hot tub, turned a lovely shade of fuchsia. "There's nothing wrong with using music to process my feelings," he huffed defensively. "Don't tell me you—never mind. Forget I said anything."

Maybe he isn't a complete idiot. Yes, Joel, I have *made breakup playlists, including after you broke my heart. It was just as shitty as you would imagine for a pissed-off and weepy teenage girl.*

She closed her eyes and listened as a tolling bell mixed with powerful drum beats and slowly building guitars as the singer wove the tale of a condemned man contemplating his all-too-brief future, trying to understand his fate before spitting defiance as he is led to the gallows. The long, building musical interlude made her feel like the doomed man's accelerating heartbeat as his end drew nigh. As the pounding beat crested, the singer howled, "Hallowed Be Thy Name," holding the last note as the pace slackened, like the last few heartbeats after the trap door opened under the condemned man's feet.

"Damn, dude."

He chuckled. "I know, right?"

They drank their beers and listened to more songs, slowly drifting closer. Eventually, Mona found herself sitting next to Joel, their submerged knees and thighs pressed against each other.

Shit. I didn't mean to get so close to him. It feels...pleasant, though. Like maybe staying like this wouldn't be the worst choice available. Or maybe the hot water and the beer are messing with my state of mind, and I should go before touching goes further. I should get out of the hot tub now, but what I really want is just one more song.

"I'm going to head inside in a minute, but first play "You Shook Me All Night Long" for me. I want to listen to something I know and can sing to."

"You got it," he responded, fiddling with his phone.

Mona felt a shiver run up her spine at the opening chord. Holding her empty beer bottle like a microphone, she belted out the lyrics, joined in a duet by Joel who mimicked her bottle microphone. They were both grinning broadly by the time the closing notes faded.

"Okay. I'm going now. See you inside."

Now I understand why strippers love this song so much. I'm horny as fuck right now.

Chapter 7

You Shook Me All Night Long
AC/DC

Mona slammed the cabin door behind her and raced for her towel hanging by the wood stove. It was hot and a bit stiff, but it felt incredible against her cold skin. She dried herself as best she could, but the t-shirt plastered to her ribcage was soaked and had chilled rapidly during her brief rush from the hot tub. Hanging her towel back up, she reached for the hem of the shirt, peeling it slowly upward, leaving a cool, damp trail across her abdomen.

The slamming of the back door caused her to arrest her movement. Joel stopped and stared at her as she held the shirt slightly below her boobs.

"Nope. You already got your one free show yesterday. Get your ass in the bathroom and shut the door."

Joel looked like a puppy with an empty food bowl. "Can I at least get my towel?"

She nodded. "Fine."

He jogged over, hauled his towel down, and dried himself off as he stepped into the compact bathroom and closed the door.

With a grateful sigh, Mona stripped off the damp shirt and boy shorts. Standing starkers in front of the wood stove, she exalted in the brief moment of freedom. She spun to warm her backside before hanging up her towel and soaked clothing on the rack next to the hot stove.

The knob on the bathroom door creaked as it turned, returning Mona's attention to her bare state. She barked out, "Joel, if you open that door, I swear I'll rip your arms off and beat you to death with them."

A muffled response came from the bathroom, but the doorknob stopped twisting. Mona bolted up the stairs and out of sight. She briefly contemplated stranding Joel inside the bathroom for the rest of the night before deciding to show mercy. Mona called downstairs, "It's safe to come out."

She threw on cozy pajama pants and a soft flannel shirt before returning to the main floor. At the halfway turn of the spiral staircase, she stopped and beheld Joel standing in front of the wood stove. He had his towel wrapped around his waist and his swim trunks dangled loosely from his fingers. Standing like a statue, he studied her wet garments where they hung on the drying rack.

"Ahem." Mona cleared her throat to break Joel's trance.

He jumped at the sound, whirling around with crimson cheeks. "Um..."

Oh yeah, he was definitely thinking of me naked. Correction, he is imagining me naked. He's standing there in a towel, which means he's naked underneath. And now I'm the one picturing him naked as well. It's not a bad image. A little doughy in the middle, but he makes it work. Damn. Now is not the time to be horny.

"I was...uh."

"You were looking for a place to hang your towel and swimsuit, right?"

"Exactly." He looked so relieved.

"You definitely weren't checking out my wet clothing and thinking of me, were you?"

Mona giggled at his guilty expression, then almost choked when his towel twitched, right where his cock would be.

"I'm going to hang up my trunks and get changed," he sputtered, cheeks and ears a balmy pink. They passed each other at the base of the stairs, and Mona resisted the urge to look up to catch a glimpse under his towel.

She plopped down in her chair with her book where she was quickly joined by a cat. Once they managed to get situated, she opened her book and tried not to think about naked humans. Her attempts to cleanse her mind were in vain as her book was a romance novel, and she was reading a rather spicy part.

Okay...what editor thought allowing the author to write a sentence including the words, "juicy schlong," was a good idea? What would make a schlong juicy anyway? A juicy pussy makes sense, but I've never considered dicks to be juicy. I wonder if...nope. I'm not going to think about Joel's johnson. Great. Trying not *to think about it means now I'm thinking about his cock again. Oh, wow. "Juicy johnson" would have been much better than "juicy schlong." Maybe I should write a romance novel.*

Joel interrupted her mental spiral as he descended the stairs. "Can I read with you and Itsabella?"

"*Hah.* I've got you saying her name now. Yes, you can join us. Obviously in your own chair." She flashed him a toothy grin, which only widened when he rolled his eyes.

"Of course. Would you like anything to drink?"

"What have we got?"

"We're running low on beer—"

Mona snorted. "*My* beer, which you keep drinking."

He had the decency to look abashed. "As I was saying, we're running low on *your* beer, but we have water, whiskey, and I can fix us tea or cocoa."

"Is it cocoa or hot chocolate?"

Joel cocked his head. "I've heard both. I'm not sure what the difference is."

"Me either, but I'd like some hot chocolate with a splash of whiskey."

"Oh," he exclaimed with widening eyes. "I like how you think."

Mona relaxed with her feet stretched out on the ottoman in front of the wood stove, Itsabella blissfully draped across her thighs, one paw stretched languidly into the air. She read while Joel puttered about, his noises coming closer. Lifting her eyes above the top of her book, she furtively observed the movement of his ass and thighs as he placed a small table between their chairs. A soft, appreciative hum escaped her lips when he strolled back into the kitchenette.

"Hey, would you like some microwave popcorn?" Joel called out.

"Sure."

A few minutes later, he placed a tray with a bowl of popcorn and two steaming mugs on the table.

"Napkins?" She asked.

"Oh, sorry. I have the table manners of an—" Cheeks flaring pink, he shut his mouth before he finished the sentence, so she completed it for him.

"—of an orc."

"Mona, I apologize. I was very rude."

"Yes, you were, although after growing up with my father and two brothers, you aren't wrong, either." She chortled as she remembered weekends watching football long ago. "They had no couth at all."

"I have no idea what to say."

"Oh, lighten up, Joel," she chided. "Yes, you made a stupid and racist comment, but it's not anything I haven't heard a thousand times before. Better than most, really."

"You're not helping."

She rolled her eyes. "Fine. Would you like to hear about the time right after Rick was drafted by Tallahassee and we found a barbeque place with an all-you-can-eat special on ribs? Between dad, Rick, and Russell, I'm pretty sure the restaurant had nothing left at the end of the night. There was a small hill of bones on the table, and the three of them were covered head to toe in grease and sauce."

A slight smile cracked his lips. "And I bet you were perfectly clean."

Mona sniffed haughtily, nose in the air. "I ate a moderate amount of ribs and used napkins, thank you very much. I'm a lady."

"Yes, you are."

Do I detect a wistful tone in his voice? I keep coming back to his possible slip up with the present tense of "I love you." He better not have feelings, because I definitely don't.

After a quick trip to the kitchenette, he handed her a sheaf of napkins and kept some for himself. They sat and read in silence, munching on popcorn and sipping their drinks. Mona occasionally petted Itsabella, who purred contentedly in response.

Eventually, Joel stood and stretched. "Comfortable?"

Mona groaned. "I was, but Itsabella is getting heavy."

"Do you want me to move her?"

"*No,*" she cried. Gesturing at the contented feline, Mona said, "look how happy she is. She's smiling in her sleep."

"Okay," he drawled. "How about I start on dinner, then? Does stir-fry sound good?"

"Heck yeah, I love stir-fry."

"What do you put in yours?"

She arched an eyebrow at him. With a tone to fully imply the obviousness of her response, she said, "It's stir-fry. I put in whatever I've got on hand."

Joel threw up his hands defensively. "Sorry, I asked."

Mona sighed and settled herself. *It's not Joel's fault that I'm horny and frustrated. We're stuck here together until the snow clears, and I can't snap at him every time I feel grumpy.* "No, I'm sorry. Everyone does their stir-fry differently."

"Mostly, I wanted to know if there's anything you didn't want."

"Mushrooms. Definitely no mushrooms."

Joel pursed his lips. "Huh." She could see a sly twinkle in his eyes, and the corners of his mouth twitched. "So, if you are what you eat, are you saying you're not a *fungi?*"

Mona glared at him, but his giggling glee cracked her frowning façade. "You're proud of your little pun, aren't you?"

"Just a tiny bit." He held up his thumb and forefinger, just slightly separated, in front of his huge grin.

She shook her head before returning to her book. Itsabella hopped off her lap at the sound of cat food in a bowl, leaving a slightly warmer spot on Mona's thighs. Her legs felt slow-roasted from the heat of the wood stove. She rubbed her legs vigorously to restore blood flow, wincing at the tingling sensations emanating from her protesting muscles before spinning her chair around to get her legs some time away from the heat.

Getting lost in the pages of her book allowed Mona to tune out the activity in the cabin and focus on the book's action unfolding in her mind's eye. Her underlying horniness wasn't helped by the impending spicy scene where the heroine was about to get down and dirty with one guy on a couch while another guy watched. Her tongue traced her lips and mandibular fangs in delightful anticipation. She was only partway through the scene when a gentle tap on her shoulder broke her reverie. Her eyes flicked up to notice Joel standing above her.

"Ready for dinner?"

Shifting her gaze to the small table, she could see a steaming pot set between two candles with a whiskey bottle to the side.

Her stomach lurched amidst a bewildering array of reactions.

Do I want a candlelight dinner with Joel? Is there some sort of plan? If there is, then he's being highly presumptuous. I should shut this down immediately, although it might be nice to have dinner with a man who makes an effort for once. It is cute. Possibly even sweet, depending on his intentions.

"What's this?" She asked in a guarded tone.

"Oh, the candles? You know, we may be stuck here for a while, and candles help the generator run less. We don't want to run out of fuel." He almost managed to look completely innocent as he said it.

"Uh-huh. Whatever. Either way, I'm hungry and your stir-fry smells wonderful."

He held out a chair for her as she approached the table, but she sauntered past him with a smirk and dropped into the other chair.

I'm not falling for your bullshit, Joel.

She heaped a heavy pile of stir-fry into her bowl and sniffed, inhaling the savory odors. Picking up her fork, she dug into the food.

"Not bad, Joel. Not bad at all."

"Thank you. I mean, it's just stir-fry. Nothing special."

"Dude. You can fix a meal from scratch and make it taste good. You're already ahead of half the country. Probably way more than half."

"So, it's good? Better than 'not bad?' Because you said—"

Mona pointed her fork at him. "I know what I said, Joel. Don't press your luck."

He mumbled, "Okay," and focused on eating. She did the same, helping herself to seconds along the way. Once finished, she cleaned her dishes in the sink and returned to her chair.

"*Itsabella,* this is my chair. You need to get up."

The cat opened one baleful eye before settling her head down on top of her paws.

Joel chuckled, adding, "Once she's settled in, she isn't going anywhere. You're going to need a new chair."

Mona harrumphed and dropped into Joel's chair.

"*Hey,* I meant a different chair."

"This *is* a different chair."

"Yes, but it's my chair."

"You know, once I'm settled in, I'm not going anywhere. You're going to need a new chair now." She flashed him a toothy, triumphant grin.

"Not cool, Mona." He hung his head in defeat and spun on his heel.

She read while Joel put away the remains of dinner. Her reading was interrupted by the involuntary nodding of her head. When she realized she was reading the same paragraph over and over again, she finally gave up.

"Okay. I'm heading to bed. Night, Joel. Night, Itsabella."

"Sleep well. Is it okay if I come up soon?"

"Whatever," she responded, trying to ignore the unwanted quickening of her pulse. "No spooning or funny business."

Upstairs, she slid into the bed and quickly drifted off to sleep. Sometime in the dead of the night, she woke up feeling seriously overheated. Slipping out of bed, she padded downstairs in near total darkness for some water before returning to the loft. As she crested the stairs, she discerned Joel sitting upright in bed, tugging off his shirt.

"Mona? Are you there?" he whispered, peering vainly into the darkness.

"I'm here. Do you need some water?" she replied.

Joel nodded. "Yeah, I'm warm and kind of thirsty."

She eyed his chest in the dark. *I've seen better, but I've seen a lot worse, and I'm kind of thirsty, too.*

"Here, take my glass, and I'll go get another for me."

"You—"

"Shut it, Joel. I can see in the dark, and you can't." She carefully pressed the glass into his outstretched hand and went downstairs for another. Returning once again, she placed her glass of water on the nightstand and lay down. She could feel him shifting on the bed.

"Mona?"

"Yeah?" She rolled onto her side to face him.

"Thank you."

"For what?"

"I messed up a long time ago, and I guess I'm just thankful you gave me the opportunity to come clean about my mistakes. It doesn't make any of what I did right, but I'm glad we talked."

"Thank you for opening up." Before her logic centers could object, she leaned forward and kissed him. Just a small peck on the lips, innocent and meaningless her higher brain functions assured themselves, but deep inside, something stirred.

As she pulled back, he placed his hand gently on her arm. He wasn't gripping her, and she could easily have pulled away, but his touch sent electric fire along her nerves. Her own hand reached out to trace languidly along his chest. She saw the burning need in his eyes and felt a reflection of the same desire blazing in her own heart.

Leaning back in, she kissed him again. No quick peck this time. Her sudden craving for his lips, his touch, was all-consuming and feral. Mona moaned and opened her lips, her tongue seeking a play-mate. It found a friendly companion inside Joel's mouth, and they began a frenzied dance.

Joel's hand strayed to her neck as his fingers slipped into her hair.

"Sorry, I should have showered earlier. My hair must be a mess," she panted as she broke their kiss.

"No, your hair is perfect," Joel responded as his hand slid down to her collarbone where its motion was arrested by her shirt.

"Fuck it," Mona growled as she picked frantically at the offending garment. Sitting up and sliding her shirt over her head, she threw it to the ground and shook out her hair. Joel stared at her in slack-jawed appreciation as a faint glimmer of moonlight illuminated her.

Grinning at the moan which escaped his throat, she dove in for another passionate kiss. A grateful groan tumbled from her own throat when Joel's fingers tweaked a bare nipple. Her body jolted forward, her bare emerald skin pressed against his pale flesh. Further down, her pajama-clad legs intertwined with his, and she felt the solid tumescence in his pants pressed against her mound. They both whined in mutual frustration.

Hands explored bare backs and flanks while their mouths danced a mutual mambo. Joel eventually broke off the kiss so he could run his tongue up her jawline until he took the jagged shape of her earlobe between his teeth. She grimaced and grunted as he pulled and gnawed on her sensitive skin in between the row of earrings. His tongue caressing her skin and jostling the metal rings sent tremors racing into her brain and groin. As he crawled up to gain a better angle on her ear, she took advantage of the opportunity to slide her hands under the back waistband of his pants.

"*Please,*" he whimpered, further expressing himself with a buck of his hips.

She dragged his pants down, reaching one hand to the front to grasp his hard cock. "*Oh*, someone's excited." Mona felt the answering anticipation between her own legs as wetness seeped down her thighs.

Joel backed down from her ear, briefly stopping at her lips before descending to her neck. Soon, his questing mouth made the short jaunt to her sensitive breasts. His tongue traced slow spirals inward to her aching areolas, trading off with teeth which grazed her pebbled nipples. She rolled onto her back, and Joel immediately latched onto one breast, sucking hard while his tongue lashed her nipple. He used his hand to cradle the underside of the other boob while his thumb and forefinger pinched her nipple. Mona moaned appreciatively when Joel rolled and twisted the nipple between his fingers.

He fumbled off his pants with the other hand while simultaneously worshiping her heaving tits. When he placed his now free hand on her hips, she understood the silent question he was asking her. The same question she was already asking of herself.

How far are each of us willing to go?

Mona knew exactly how far her body wanted to go, and in this moment, her raging hormones were calling all the shots. She placed a hand over his and together, they slid her pants off. Sliding one leg underneath him, she helped him align himself with her.

Her rational mind finally managed to break through the blizzard of lust for a brief instant. "Do you have a condom?"

Joel hesitated above her. "I wasn't expecting anyone to be here, so no, I didn't bring any. You?"

"Same. I was supposed to be alone."

He pulled back. "What do you want to do?"

"Are you clean?"

"Yes. I got tested after Cheri…" She could see the embarrassment on his face at the mention of his ex-wife's name.

Mona pulled him in for a kiss and they melted together. "I'm on the pill, just fuck me."

"I…"

"Joel, don't make me change my mind."

"On it."

"Yeah, you are," she purred. She forestalled any further conversation, reaching up with one hand to firmly grasp Joel's neck and draw his mouth down to hers once more. With her other hand, she took hold of his cock and guided him to her entrance. She rubbed the tip along her lips, letting his precum and her dripping juices mingle to ease his entry.

Hooking her heels behind Joel's thighs, she urged him forward. They groaned into each other's mouths as the head slipped inside. They both grunted in mutual frustration as everything ground to a halt. Joel drew back slightly while Mona drew in a deep breath. He pushed forward, and she expelled her breath and relaxed. Joel slid in a bit deeper this time.

"It's been a while for me," Mona whispered.

"Me, too," Joel replied. "But we're getting there."

He pulled back again as she drew in another breath. As Joel thrust firmly, but gently forward again, Mona groaned, "We're definitely getting there." They repeated the process again, and the resistance suddenly disappeared. Mona grunted into his mouth when he collided delightfully with her clit. She felt stretched and full in a wonderful way.

"*Oh, fuck.* You feel good inside me."

"You're..." Joel held still as his brain appeared to short circuit. "...amazing." He kissed her again before he began to move, slowly building up speed like a locomotive accelerating away from the station. Each backstroke left her craving more. She enthusiastically met each thrust with her rising hips. He lowered his head to nibble her neck as he continued to rock his hips back and forth

"Joel, this feels great, but I need you to pound me into the fucking mattress."

"Uh huh," he grunted as he picked up his pace. As ordered, he hammered her relentlessly, sending shockwave after shockwave through her thighs and up her spine.

Mona kept one hand around his neck while the other fingered her clit. Primed by her earlier horniness and stimulated inside and out, she felt her climax building rapidly. With a keening moan, she tightened her grip on Joel as she came. Riding the afterglow of her orgasm, she kissed Joel, tasting the sweat beading on his upper lip.

She could feel him falter and struggle, his energy spent from bringing her to orgasm. Mona pushed Joel back, and he collapsed onto the bed with a whimper. On shaking legs, she straddled him and sank down onto his cock. Wearily, she rode him until she felt him stiffen inside her. With a cry of his own, he followed her into ecstasy.

They lay joined together as aftershocks quivered through their bodies. Their kisses were no longer frenzied with lust, but instead were tender and gentle. Eventually, they separated wearily and rolled out of the growing wet spot to fall asleep.

Chapter 8

Tornado Warnings

Sabrina Carpenter

Joel woke up to something striking his face. His sleep-addled mind tried to make sense of something warm, soft, and somewhat fuzzy impacting his chin and mouth with gentle yet insistent force. After three or four more nudges, he grudgingly opened his eyes in time for Itsabella to slip her sandpapery tongue along his lips and nose. He shuddered and fought the urge to scream. He wiped his hand over his mouth to try to cleanse the thought of the cat slobber slathered on his face, especially since he knew where Itsabella's tongue had been when she groomed herself.

"Shh. Okay, girl," he whispered. "I'm getting up. What time is it? Never mind, just don't wake Mona." He managed to swing his legs over the side of the bed into the chill morning air before boosting himself into a sitting position around the insistent cat.

Itsabella waited until Joel was fully upright before bounding off the bed to land with a soft thump.

"Thanks, Bitsy," he grumbled. "You couldn't have gotten off the bed twenty seconds ago to make it easier for me?"

The cat ignored him as she flounced down the spiral staircase. He tugged on his discarded sweatpants from the night before and followed her.

Joel knew he'd need to feed her soon before she started crying, but he stopped at the wood stove first. He added a log, then stuffed some kindling under it, which caught fire on the embers. He watched until the log began to burn, reveling in the growing heat.

Satisfied, he closed the grate and stood up to feed Itsabella. She paced in agitated ellipses, getting underfoot as he reached for her bowl. "You're making this harder," he hissed. Itsabella ignored him.

Once he finished taking care of Itsabella's needs, he took care of his own. He pondered making coffee, but decided to wait rather than risk waking Mona. Instead, he settled for cold water. Drink in hand, he sat down in his chair with his borrowed book, and Itsabella hopped in his lap.

Or, I could go up into the loft and see what Mona thinks about morning sex. Probably not wise. I'll wait until she's actually awake before I bring up the possibility of another round. I certainly wasn't expecting anything to happen last night, but I enjoyed our time immensely. Hopefully, she feels the same way.

His internal discussion was halted when Mona appeared on the stairs. He stared slack-jawed as she descended. Her dark hair was rumpled and messy, and the ivory of her pair of fangs poking up from her lips contrasted against the mossy green color of her skin. Her flannel shirt and pajama pants were wrinkled and a slight gap flashing skin and tattoos appeared then disappeared as she walked.

Wow. She is beautiful. Absolutely radiant. Shakespeare could probably compose something truly brilliant to describe. "But soft, what light through yonder window breaks? It is the East, and Mona is the sun." Here's hoping we end up better off than Romeo and Juliet did.

Mona grumbled, "What are you staring at?"

"You." He couldn't stifle a grin. "You look incredible."

"Fuck off. I look like shit."

"Seriously, I've never seen a more beautiful woman."

Mona grunted. "Coffee?"

"I haven't made any yet. I didn't want to wake you."

She snapped her fangs in irritation. "You banging around down here was more than enough to wake the dead."

He felt his cheeks flush with hot blood. "I tried to be quiet."

"Yeah, well. You weren't," she growled.

"I'm sorry. I didn't mean to wake you. I feel as if I've upset you."

She ignored him, focusing on the coffee maker instead.

Joel awkwardly lifted a protesting Itsabella out of his lap so he could walk over to Mona. "Have I done something to upset you?"

"I'm fine," she responded, staring at her mug and not bothering to turn her head.

"I'm fine" being the universal code for "I am not fine at all." She seems pissed. Likely pissed at me. Was the sex bad? No, this seems to be much deeper.

"Well, if there's anything you want to talk about, I'm here for you."

Mona whirled around and jabbed her finger at his chest. "Of course you're here, *Joel*." His name sounded like an obscenity when she said it. "Where the hell else would you be?" She waved her arms at the snow-covered vista beyond the kitchen window. "We're stuck together in this goddess-forsaken cabin for who knows how long."

"We can try and make the best of it." He smiled, hoping she would return the gesture.

She threw her hands in the air. "Oh, sure. Like when you fucked me in the middle of the night. Are you imagining we'll make the best of it by spending the next few days fucking like rabbits before we go our separate ways again?"

"No." Joel's heart rate accelerated like a Formula One race car, and he felt beads of cold sweat pop on his forehead and palms.

Her eyes narrowed into dark slits. "Liar," she hissed.

"I mean yes—I enjoyed the sex, and I would like to do it again." He held up a hand to forestall Mona's impending explosion. "Look, this is all new and unexpected. For both of us, I imagine. It's just..."

"Just what?"

Joel looked into Mona's amethyst eyes, searching for a spark of something besides anger there. In a soft whisper, he replied, "Maybe I don't want us to go our separate ways."

"*Right*," Mona sneered. "You're just going to ignore your parents and society at large?"

His voice grew heated. "Screw my parents." Joel tapped his chest with his fist. "They don't control me anymore. As for society—why do I care what anyone else thinks?"

"Because everyone eventually cares, Joel." The heat in Mona's voice faded into weariness. "It's easy for you to say these things *now*. You might even mean it while we're stuck here in the middle of nowhere, but out there in the real world, you'll eventually come to your senses. You'll just be another in a long line of humans who like the allure of going green until the reality of what dating an orc *really* entails hits home."

"Maybe you can enlighten me, then."

"Fuck off," Mona grunted. She whirled away from him and focused on making breakfast for herself, acting as if Joel wasn't even there. After a couple awkward minutes, he retreated to his chair.

I'm going to give her some space for a bit. Whatever is going on with her involves a strong emotional reaction which I suspect stems from some combination of lived experience and trauma. I want to delve into this and understand, but I don't want to cause her additional pain. I hope she'll be more willing to talk later.

Itsabella rubbed herself against his ankles before hopping into Mona's lap when she sat down at the dining table. Joel observed Mona lift Bitsy down, but the persistent cat merely jumped right back up into her lap. He smiled to himself as Mona began stroking the purring feline and her mass of soft fur.

She's such a good cat. Her sense of who is in distress is impeccable, and she immediately responds with cat therapy. As angry as Mona is right now, it's hard to stay mad when you're getting snuggled by Itsabella.

He turned back to his book and read, patiently waiting for Mona to finish her breakfast. She didn't choose to engage with him, instead returning upstairs. Joel sighed, wallowing a bit in his disappointment. Isabella curled around his ankles. He reached down to pet her and she thrummed happily in response.

The stairs creaked above him, and Joel peeked up to observe Mona descending wearing a sleeveless shirt and baggy shorts. He pretended to read his book while she began exercising. His eyes followed the stretches and contractions of her muscles as she flowed from one exercise to the next. Joel closed his eyes and inhaled deeply, held his breath, then slowly exhaled.

He focused on reading and tuned out Mona. Joel was lost in his story until he was roused by a loud thump from the wall behind him and a snarling scream of rage.

"I can't deal with this shit," Mona roared. "I need to get out and away from you. I came here to be alone, and you've ruined everything."

He stood, holding his hands out and away from his body in a way he hoped was non-threatening. "I'm sorry I've messed up your retreat, and I understand why you want to get away from me. Perhaps we might work together to solve this challenge."

"How?" Her amethyst eyes narrowed into slits and her fangs were fully exposed.

"We could each grab a snow shovel and see what we can do to clear a way out."

"Shoveling snow? *That's* your solution?"

"Yes, actually. If you want to get out, then we need to gauge how deep the snow is and if we can clear a path. Also, the act of shoveling will burn up a shitload of energy, which—since the apparent alternative is punching my walls—might be a more productive outlet."

Mona frowned, but nodded. "Makes sense," she grumbled. "Let me get dressed." Mona climbed upstairs, leaving Joel to have a staring contest with the cat.

"What?" he exclaimed. "I'm doing my best."

Itsabella didn't respond. She just dropped to the floor and began grooming a paw.

Once Mona was dressed, Joel changed as well, meeting her outside. She was reclearing the pathway he'd dug out previously. Wind drifts and a dusting of fresh snow had erased some of his earlier effort, but there was still a path to the vehicles. The two of them quickly restored the clear tract.

Leaning on his shovel, Joel asked, "What do you think? It's about a quarter mile or so to the highway. Maybe a half mile. Either way, we have a lot of shoveling ahead of us."

"I think we should walk down to the road and see how bad it is."

"It'll be tough to walk through the snow."

Mona snorted at him. "Fine. I'll go by myself."

"Absolutely not. If something happens..." Joel let the sentence die, not wanting to delve into what ifs.

"Whatever. You can come with me or not, but don't slow me down."

He could hear the condescension in her voice, but he chose to ignore it. Instead, he hefted his snow shovel over his shoulder, nodded, and responded, "Let's go."

The trek to the road through knee-high snow had Joel quickly regretting his life choices. Mona seemed unbothered, plowing relentlessly forward while he fell ever further behind. His breath puffed in silver clouds as his chest heaved from the strain. He was questioning whether he would survive this trek when they finally reached the road.

Holy shit. There's so much snow. We're going to be here a while.

The snow and ice was almost waist deep at the side of the road, with a slurried debris field spread further back.

The plows buried our exit. I can't blame them, but this is going to be a pain in the ass to clear.

Mona was already shoveling by the time he made it to the roadside. Joining her, he dug his shovel into the snow and ice, arms and back straining as he heaved a shovelful of the heavy mass to the side. Between the two of them, it took over an hour to mostly clear the entryway. There was enough space for his car to get out, but it was still an open question of whether his car could make the drive from the cabin to the main road.

Leaning on his shovel, he asked, "Hey, do you want to head back?"

"Are you tired?" Mona asked with a sneer.

He nodded, too tired to argue. "Yes, and we've done about all we can do here."

She sniffed as she whirled around before marching back up the snow-covered access road. With a heavy sigh, he trudged behind her, once again falling further back.

Joel was about twenty paces behind Mona when she suddenly pitched face first into the snow. Adrenaline surged into his bloodstream when she didn't get up. Rushing forward, he almost tripped on a branch hidden under the frozen blanket of white powder. He maintained his balance and knelt beside her.

"Mona?"

He could see a small red stain in the snow near her ear. Joel desperately thought back to a first aid training course he'd taken a few years before, but he couldn't remember much. In his hazy memory, he recalled moving someone with a head wound was a bad idea.

"Shit. Fuck. Shit. Fuck."

"Wuh?"

Relief flooded his mind and voice. "Mona? Are you okay?"

"Why am I cold?"

"You fell."

She tried lifting herself up and he held on to support her. Mona managed to get herself to a kneeling position before she reached up to touch her temple. Her green fingers came away scarlet with new blood.

"Here." Joel pulled off his scarf and wrapped it tightly around Mona's head. "Let's get you back to the cabin so we can put on some disinfectant and bandages."

"Cold."

Her gloves were gone, probably buried under the snow. Joel leaned their shovels against a tree before helping Mona struggle to her feet. She leaned on him as they staggered up the road toward the cabin.

I don't think we're too far away. I hope not. I'm already exhausted, and she's heavy and getting heavier. We need to get back before her hypothermia gets too bad. Hopefully, she can stay upright, because I'm not sure I can drag her.

Joel's silent prayers were answered when he glimpsed the cabin through the trees ahead. "Just a little farther, Mona," he said, urging her onward. "We're almost there."

"Tired. Need...to...rest." She was beginning to slur her words.

"In a little bit. You've got this."

She tried to slow down. "Go on. I'll catch up."

"Mona. I'm not leaving you." He injected as much desperate urgency into his voice as he could in an effort to spur her onward. "I'm *never* leaving you again. Come on."

Joel hooked his arms tighter around Mona, half dragging her even as his knees threatened to buckle with each step. He kept putting one foot in front of the other, cajoling her to keep going. When his foot broke out of the snowpack and into the cleared area around his car, he felt a surge of relief. Now mostly hauling Mona, he maneuvered her up the stairs and inside the cabin.

Once inside, Joel nudged Mona over next to the stove. He said a silent prayer of thanks to any listening deity that the fire still burned. Joel tossed in a couple more split logs, and quickly felt the heat increase as they blazed. Mona didn't seem to be affected by the growing warmth as she swayed, her teeth chattering.

The long-ago memories of his first aid class resurfaced, particularly around treating hypothermia. He was about to experience the lifelong dream of his thirteen-year-old Boy Scout self, but somehow the terror gripping his heart crushed any lingering prepubescent joy. Gritting his teeth, Joel began to peel Mona's wet clothing off her trembling body. He threw a blanket around her once she was naked before stripping off his own clothes.

He threw another log in the wood stove, which was already radiating tremendous heat. Leading Mona upstairs, he managed to get her into the bed, joining her and pulling the heap of blankets on top of them. She felt cold, and he did his best to use his body heat and gentle massaging to coax warmth back into her skin.

Over time, her teeth stopped chattering, and their cocoon of blankets grew hot. Joel stroked Mona's hair and held her close, ignoring his own stiff biological reaction. Eventually, she fell asleep in his arms.

Feeling hopeful about Mona's condition, Joel extricated himself from the bed and tiptoed downstairs to get the first aid kit. He returned to the loft and gingerly cleaned the clotted blood on her temple before applying a bandage. She stirred, but remained asleep.

I hope she doesn't have a concussion. I'm way out of my element here, and there's not much chance I can get her to a hospital. We'll have to hope for the best.

He put the first aid kit down and crawled back into bed with Mona. Itsabella jumped onto the bed and nosed around at the blankets. Joel dutifully lifted the covers so she could crawl underneath to join them. Before long, he was asleep as well.

97

Chapter 9

Victim of Changes

Judas Priest

Mona felt Joel's hard cock pressed into the crack of her ass as she drifted out of sleep. His arm was draped across her tits, and there was another hot mass pressed against her stomach. Her stirring mind delved into her dim memories to pierce together why she was in this situation.

Okay, I remember arguing with Joel before I punched the wall. Then, we walked to the road and shoveled out the plow debris. We walked back and somewhere along the way, I tripped and fell.

She slowly reached up to touch her head, fingering the bandage there.

I definitely hit my head. Which doesn't explain why we're in bed...again. And naked...again. Which brings up my moment of weakness last night. Was it last night? Whatever. Why exactly did

98

I let Joel fuck me? Did I let him, or did I initiate it? Kind of mutual, I think, which doesn't make it better. I've slept with him twice in my life, and both times it's led to heartbreak.

The logical part of Mona's brain objected to her line of reasoning.

Has it led to misery and woe this time?

Not yet, but it will.

Maybe it won't. Joel isn't seventeen anymore.

No, he's not. This time the sex was good. Even Pessimistic Mona was impressed.

Logical Mona responded. *He's had fifteen years to improve. I should hope so.*

Great, fifteen years of sleeping around so he can be a better lay this time around.

Oh, like we were a nun during those years. I seem to recall us fucking a respectable number of people across both species and gender lines.

Pessimistic Mona was unswayed. *Back to my point—whatever this was last night, it is inevitably doomed.*

Admittedly, our history suggests an unavoidable wretchedness; however, past experience is not necessarily indicative of future results.

What the fuck? Spare us the bullshit sales pitch.

Logical Mona tried a different tack. *He said he loves us—present tense.*

Ugh. Slip of the tongue.

Mmm, he definitely slipped us some tongue last night. And a hard cock.

Hang on. Aren't you the logical part of my head?

I'm still us. Or is it we?

Mona was saved from further internal debate when the hot mass against her stomach unwound itself and crawled up to bonk her chin.

"Hello, Itsabella," she whispered. "Do you know why I'm naked?"

The cat purred and bonked her chin again.

"Not helpful, little itsy Bitsy." Mona scratched her feline friend, who responded by happily rubbing her head on the point of Mona's chin.

Their reverie was interrupted by a staccato fart from Joel, who mumbled, "Oh yeah," in his sleep.

"Ugh. Nope. I'm out of here." Mona nudged the cat. "Come on, Itsabella. Let's leave your disgusting human to stew in his own foul stench."

Extricating herself from Joel's somnolent embrace took some work—an effort made more daunting by the tempting presence of the tumescent cock lodged in the valley of her butt crack. Each time she shifted, it sent conflicting signals to her brain and her suddenly sodden pussy.

Once free, she slipped on pajama pants and a tank top before padding downstairs. She was greeted by the fading radiance of the wood stove and twin piles of damp clothing. Mona stirred the ashes inside the stove and added a fresh log to stave off the chill beginning to develop inside the cabin. She tidied up the clothes, hanging them to finish drying while pondering her missing gloves.

I must have lost them in the snow outside. Did Joel get me back to the cabin? Was I hypothermic? Hypothermia would explain a lot *about my recent sleeping arrangements. I wonder if I can get a weather report on the little radio in the kitchenette.*

She flicked the radio on and turned the volume down, listening while she put a saucepan of water on the stove to heat and pulled out a can of food for Itsabella. The big cat circled her legs, crying desperately as she peeled back the lid of the can and scooped food into the bowl. "Too bad you don't have thumbs, little one."

Itsabella reared up onto her hind legs in a frantic dance as Mona set the bowl down. She listened to the contented gobbling noises while she emptied a packet of hot chocolate mix into a mug, followed by hot water. Mona stirred it up and sighed after taking a sip.

"Hey."

Startled, Mona spun to find Joel leaning on the railing of the spiral staircase wearing boxer briefs and a t-shirt.

"Hey," she said back.

"Mona, I'm sorry about earlier, it's just—"

"You were saving my life?"

He reached his arm up and behind to scratch the back of his neck, with a sheepish expression on his face. "Yeah. Pretty much."

In a quiet voice, she asked, "How bad was it?"

"I was worried. Really worried." Joel shuddered from head to toe. "Okay, I was panicking because you were slowing down. If you'd stopped, I don't think I could have carried you. Just when I thought you might give up on me, we made it to the cabin, and everything was okay." He smiled at her. "How does your head feel? And your toes."

She mentally assessed herself and flexed her various digits. "My head is as good as ever. We orcs have thick skulls. My fingers and toes all seem to be in working condition."

"Do you mind if I check for patches of dead skin? I seem to recall something from my first aid training, but it's been so many years."

Mona held her hands up. "My fingers are fine, but you can check my toes. I don't want any damage if I'm going to make money on OnlyFeet."

Joel snorted and laughed at the same time. "I'm sorry—what?"

"I..." The tufted tops of her ears bristled.

The corners of his mouth quivered, and his eyes danced gleefully. "Oh, come on. You can tell me."

"I probably shouldn't."

"Then don't say anything. Let me guess..." Joel chuckled again. "Tiffany talked you into something, and you're not entirely sold on it yet."

"Yeah. She said I could probably make good money from guys ogling my toes on OnlyFeet." Mona's ear tufts were shaking now, and her cheeks heated. "Okay, we both know they'd be doing more than ogling." Her hand mimed stroking a shaft.

She could see Joel's shoulders shiver from unvoiced laughter. "At least Tiff didn't talk you into doing porn." His head cocked to one side. "Or did she?"

Mona shook her head vigorously. "No. I'm pretty sure porn would not go well for me."

"Dare I ask why?"

"Have you ever watched orc porn?" She felt her eyebrows rising.

Joel's face brightened into a splendid shade of scarlet. "Uhh."

"Clearly that's a yes. Were the orcs in question guys or girls?"

"Mostly orc dudes with human or sometimes elf chicks."

"None with orc women?"

"I saw bits of a few with orc actresses, but those were super abusive and gross." Joel stuck his tongue out and shuddered in disgust. "I quit watching immediately."

Mona sighed. "Exactly. For whatever reason, there's a whole fetish kink about human or elf women 'going green' but not the reverse. I'm not exactly a connoisseur, but from what I've heard, most porn involving orcs tends to be massively degrading, and I'm not interested."

He nodded sagely. "Understandable. You're a strong and beautiful woman. You deserve better."

"Quit with the bullshit flattery, Joel."

"I'm being sincere, but you know what—I'll shut up now."

"Anyway, Tiff talked me into OnlyFeet, but nothing else. I could use the money."

"Well, let me check your money makers, then."

Mona sat on her favorite chair and set her feet on the ottoman. Joel knelt down to poke and caress her soles and toes. "Mmm, feel free to give me a foot massage while you're down there," she said with a broad grin.

"My pleasure," he responded before digging his knuckles into the sole of her right foot. "Your feet look fine to me. Obviously, I'm not an expert, but I don't see any patches of dead skin down there."

"Oh...good...yes...good."

She heard him chuckle softly as his hands worked their magic.

"Can I ask you about your tattoos?" His expression was eager, even as his hands kept busy.

"What do you want to know?"

"Is there any special meaning around them?"

Mona stared at him for a minute or so as she formulated a response. "I have a lot of tattoos."

"I noticed," he shot back with a toothy grin.

She grimaced in response. "Some of them have meaning, some don't. Mostly, I..." Mona sighed. "How do I explain this? I'm an orc, and we live at the mercy of humans and elves. Because only the shittiest jobs are generally open to orcs, I'm usually poor, and I've had landlords kick me out even when I was paid up on my rent because they wanted to rent to a 'better clientele.' So, at any time, all of my belongings could end up on the street or in the dumpster. I've learned to live with limited possessions. One of my passions is art, and since any paintings or prints I own could be trashed at any time, instead I wear the art I love."

Joel's expression shifted as she spoke, morphing from a cheerful grin to a somber frown to an angry grimace. Mona felt her own familiar rage rising as well.

"*Holy shit,*" he cried. "I'm so sorry."

"Fuck your sorry," she spat. "Saying 'sorry' doesn't do shit. You know what does? Voting. Organizing. Spreading the word. *Use your fucking privilege for good.* Get educated, you twatwaffle. Listen, learn, have some empathy, and then *do* something."

"I will." He returned to kneading her foot in his hands, which made storming off dramatically impossible. "Mona?"

"What, Joel?" She couldn't keep the irritation out of her voice. Her mood was further darkened by the pleasant sensations of the foot massage as it was interfering with her righteous rage.

"Thank you for being open and honest with me."

Her mind cataloged a vast number of potential responses to his statement, yet she remained silent. Instead she observed him sitting on the ottoman with her left heel cupped in one hand, while the other pressed firmly into the balls of her foot. The whole time, Joel kept his eyes focused on her face while a smile crept stealthily onto his lips like a burglar tiptoeing past a dozing security guard.

"What are you grinning about?"

"Sorry." He paused and cocked his head. "Actually, no. I'm not sorry."

"Hmm?"

"Okay, please let me finish before you kick my ass. It's complicated. I'm very sorry about the shit you've dealt with in your life because of being born an orc. At the same time, I admire your grit, determination, and intelligence. You are an inspiring person and thoroughly beautiful on so many levels."

"Now you're just trying to get into my pants again."

"I mean..." He had the grace to have the embarrassed and panicked look of a kid who'd just hit a baseball through the neighbor's window. "Yes, I would very much enjoy more time in your trousers, but I'm not complimenting you because I want to get laid again."

"Uh-huh." She made sure her tone fully expressed her disbelief.

"It's true, Mona. Look, I may not have all the answers about society, or my parents, or Tiffany—"

"*Oh, fuck.*" Mona sat upright, nearly yanking her foot out of Joel's hands.

"What?"

"I slept with my best friend's brother."

"Which is bad?"

"*Yes,* you idiot," she growled. "Do you not understand Girl Code?"

"Uhh."

Tiff seemed okay with it back in high school. Well, she was fine with me dating Joel back then, although she never said anything about us getting it on. At least she was supportive after he ditched me. She never slut shamed me. A lot has changed, though. She's no longer daydreaming about us being sisters forever. Also, she tried...

"Fucking hells."

Joel had been staring at her while her mind reeled, his hands never stopping their kneading on her feet. "Uh oh. What now?"

"After I got fired, Tiff and I slept together." She saw his eyebrows climbing his forehead. "As in, sleeping, not screwing," Mona growled.

"Wait...what's the big deal, then?"

Men. As intelligent as a box of rocks, and just as emotionally aware.

With a heavy and abundantly meaningful sigh, she responded, "Because, she sort of offered to have sex with me."

His hands stopped kneading and his mouth formed an 'O' big enough to drive a bus through. "She did? But you... My sister's a lesbian?"

"Seriously?" She shook her head. "Tiff is very open-minded and has dated across the spectrum. As have I."

"Oh." Joel looked like someone suffering from severe constipation as his mind seemingly struggled to process new information. "So, are you two...together?"

She shot back sternly, "We're friends, and Tiff's offer was made out of friendship. As beautiful and amazing as Tiffany is, I'm perfectly happy remaining platonic friends with her."

Well, she told me it was an offer as a friend helping out a friend going through a rough patch. What if Tiff wasn't being fully honest? If she did want more, would I want it as well? Have I screwed our relationship up by banging her brother? I should have learned this lesson fifteen years ago. I did learn this lesson then. I just forgot it in a weak moment. You know what isn't weak? His hands. Goddess, I love a good foot massage. He looks sexy down there, and he's been taking good care of me. Oh, right. He's still my best friend's brother, and the man who broke my heart.

"You still look confused," she said.

Goddess knows I'm confused, too.

"Probably because I am." Joel let out a low chuckle. "I feel way out of my depth right now. Honestly, I'm pretty sure the kiddie pool might be too deep for me at this moment. The one thing I'm certain of is that I don't want to mess things up, especially with us."

"There is no *us,* Joel."

But what if there could be?

"I know." He fought the frown on his lips, turning it into a smile which never quite reached his eyes. "Are you hungry?"

At the mention of food, Mona's stomach rumbled like a rickety old roller coaster as it rounded a bend.

"Sounds like a 'yes,' then. Mac and chili sound good?"

"Goddess, please."

She managed to contain a disappointed whimper when he put her feet down and stood up. Her grumbling stomach aside, Mona felt surprisingly good for being on death's door earlier in the day.

*For which I need to thank Joel, even if I don't want to. There's one way I could thank him——him and his hard cock. Nope. Don't go there. Joel broke your heart, and he's your best friend's brother. On the other hand, he felt so fucking good nestled naked against you with his juicy schlong pressed...*fuck. *Damn whoever wrote that stupid phrase in a book. Also, I'm supposed to be finding reasons* not *to shag him again. We're stuck together in this cabin for another day, at least. I could just enjoy myself...and him. It's just a physical release. It doesn't have to be anything more.*

With a wanton grin to match her ribald thoughts, she gripped the arms of the chair and levered herself upright before climbing the stairs.

Chapter 10

Physical

Dua Lipa

Joel tapped a bit of black pepper and garlic powder into the mac before giving it a vigorous final stirring. He carried it to the table and set it down carefully. Hearing steps behind him, he spun around just in time to gawk as Mona descended the final few steps. His breath caught in his throat.

She'd changed into a long flannel shirt whose bottom hem reached the upper portion of her well-muscled thighs. Below her shirt was an enthralling expanse of green skin and black ink which ended at long socks extending above the knee.

"Thank you for checking on my feet earlier. And the wonderful massage, of course," she said.

"Uh."

Great response, Joel. Get your shit together. I know it's hard…oh yeah, it's hard all right. Fucking idiot. Stop thinking with your dick. Also, stop thinking like a dick.

Snapping his mouth closed so he didn't look like a surprised trout, Joel managed to settle himself enough for a coherent response. "You're welcome. I'm glad you're not injured and are feeling better."

"Me too. Dinner looks *yummy*," Mona purred.

"It should. Honestly, you did the hard part with the chili. I just made mac and cheese from a box. Again. So the credit should go to you."

"Flatterer." She was smiling as she said it, and her eyes twinkled under hooded eyelashes, sending a nearly debilitating surge of blood into his erogenous zones.

"Something to drink?" He asked, desperately trying to recall the last ten winners of the World Series. *The Yankees won recently, right? It couldn't have been the Mets. Dodgers? Red Sox? Didn't someone cheat a few years ago? Does it still count if the team cheated?*

To his unrepentantly rigid cock, he thought, *"Come on, I just need you to go down."*

"Water, thanks," Mona replied, her voice tinkling like a diminutive waterfall.

She knows I'm struggling, and she's enjoying every second of it. I'm not sure why she's decided to torment me, but it's working. When did the Blue Jays last win the Series? What about one of those teams in Florida? Baseball isn't helping. Maybe I could think of Margaret Thatcher in leather.

He adjusted himself surreptitiously as he filled two water glasses, hoping his still-solid erection might not be too visible. One look at Mona's face dashed any optimism he entertained. She leered at his bulge as he approached the table.

"Thank you again for working so *hard* on dinner."

Joel chose not to engage with Mona's innuendo. "You're welcome. Like I said, it was mostly you. Either way, I hope everything is tasty."

Am I missing something, or is there an extra button on her shirt undone?

He turned on the small radio before sitting down. They listened to music as they ate, chatting idly about the irritation of endless holiday commercials during the breaks. Silence reigned when the weather report came on.

"A dusting of snow at our elevation up to maybe a couple of inches. I'm hoping for something on the lighter side," Mona opined.

Joel felt disappointment creep in like a mouse emerging from a hole to seek food. He tamped down his feelings and settled on an agreeable response. "Me too. I'll shovel more snow tomorrow. Do you think you'll be okay to help?"

"I should be fine shoveling snow. I'm looking forward to getting the hell out of here."

And I'm dreading the prospect of losing Mona before I figure out what my feelings are. I think I still love her. Actually, I'm pretty damn sure of it. I'm just too much of a coward to tell her.

"Yeah," he said with as much ersatz bravado he could muster. "Getting out of here would be great."

She nodded. "Yep."

"After I do the dishes, I might use the hot tub one last time. Since we're leaving tomorrow and all."

Mona flashed a toothy grin. "Hey, you made dinner. Why don't I do the dishes?"

"Wow. Thank you."

He put on his swim trunks and sat in the hot tub for a while, enjoying the winter solitude as much as his brain would allow. In the shifting border between the warm water and frigid air, his mind raced.

Mona has made it abundantly clear that she resents my prior actions and doesn't see a future for us. How I treated her when we were teenagers was reprehensible, and I completely agree with her. Then again, we've all changed and grown since then, and we're not the same people we were. Which leads into the future and what could be.

Joel drummed his fingers on the edge of the hot tub as he organized his thoughts. He idly watched snowflakes descend, glittering in the lights.

She has strong feelings about this, which I assume are based on her experiences, including with me. Chances are, I'm probably too optimistic. We need to explore this more. I want her to open up about her reasons while fully listening. She could very well be right about any relationship between us being doomed from the start.

Also, I need to figure my shit out. I just got divorced. I'm moving back to my hometown, where I'll need to rebuild my life and start a new business. Is a relationship a distraction I don't need right now?

Am I even in a good place for dating someone immediately after a divorce? Fuck it, I need to talk to her.

Joel hopped out of the hot tub, quickly covering it up before racing inside. He bolted inside the tiny bathroom to dry off and remove his wet swim trunks. Pulling on dry pajama pants, he walked into the main cabin area to hang up his dripping suit near the wood stove. He noted Mona splayed out in her chair, feet on the ottoman, with Itsabella curled in her lap. She rested her book on the sleeping cat's back.

"Can we talk?"

Her eyebrows peaked in alpine majesty. "About?"

"Us."

"Didn't we talk about this earlier?"

"No. I feel like our previous conversation was very one-sided."

Itsabella's head popped up with a quizzical squeak as Mona opened her legs, revealing her uncovered pussy. "We *could* talk. Or..." She flashed him a lascivious grin.

He fought to keep his gaze above her abdomen with limited success.

"Sorry. Didn't you say earlier—"

"Joel," she barked. Continuing in an exasperated tone, she asked, "Why do you keep bringing up things I said before? Are you *trying* to make this complicated? We're two horny adults snowed in at a cabin. You have a limited time to accept this offer. If my legs close before you say 'yes,' then you're not getting any." She punctuated her final sentence by slowly moving her legs together.

I desperately want to talk about our relationship, but holy shit, I'd be an idiot to pass this up. Fuck. Her knees are almost together.

"Okay, okay. Yes, we don't need to talk right now," he gasped, hoping he wasn't too late.

Mona's fangy grin and widening knees suggested Joel made his decision just in time. Annoyed by all the motion below her, Itsabella stood up and shook out her fluff in a huff before jumping to the floor. "At least now I don't have to feel bad about moving her," Mona commented as she stood up.

He followed her as she walked to the spiral staircase. She subtly lifted her shirt as she ascended, providing him with tantalizing glimpses of her taut green butt and glistening pussy. His erection tented the front of his pajama pants, and he didn't even bother to cover up.

Once in the loft, she whirled to face him as her hands reached for the buttons of her shirt, pulling them slowly apart to bare her breasts. "Do you like them?" She teased, her contralto voice driving his pulse upward.

Joel glided forward wordlessly into Mona's personal space to kiss her. He said huskily, "I like all of you." His hands slid up to pull her shirt off her shoulders as she unbuttoned the final button. Her hands trailed down to his waistband while he ran his tongue along her fangs.

"Uh uh," he growled as he nudged her body backward. Mona fell back onto the bed with a surprised huff. Joel eyed her captivating body, dressed only in those tall socks, with hunger. "You get my cock later. I have other plans for you right now."

"Oh?"

He knelt at the side of the bed, hooked his arms under her knees, and yanked her toward him. Up close, he savored the view between her legs, studying how her dark viridian skin tone faded to the greenish-white of a honeydew near her seeping slit. Unable to resist any longer, he dipped his head to run his tongue in a long, slow stroke from the bottom of those luscious lower lips to the hardening nub at the top. She moaned as he repeated the journey.

His hands caressed and massaged her inner thighs while he pleasured her petals with slow and sensuous strokes of his tongue.

"Oh, *fuck*, Joel," she groaned. He felt a tremor run up her thick, muscled thighs and grinned. Each long stroke of his tongue elicited additional whimpers of pleasure. "*Please.* I need...it's..."

At the top of the next stroke, Joel stayed there, pushing his face forward. His tongue lashed her emerald jewel while his nose and chin pressed into the spongy flesh above and below. He ignored the raven-black hair of her mons tickling his nostrils as he drummed a steady rhythm on her swollen clit.

Mona mewled and cooed in response, but Joel felt his tongue beginning to tire. He descended once more, nibbling and sucking on her meaty velvet curtain while he recovered. Once recuperated, he returned to pleasure her clit while also slipping two hooked fingers inside her steamy core. She cried out as he stroked her pleasure center from inside and out.

Her thighs quivered against his shoulders as her body arched and convulsed. He fought desperately to maintain his grip on her center as she shattered around him. A burst of liquid squirted against his chin, surprising him. Recovering quickly, he returned to pleasuring her while she howled in appreciation.

He felt her hands on his head, pushing him backward as her body slumped. Rocking back on his heels, Joel surveyed his handiwork. Creamy fluid slicked his fingers and seeped from her swollen lips. Her breasts heaved and jiggled with each desperate pant. A fine sheen of sweat coated her taut evergreen skin.

She reached out with crooked fingers and beckoned him to the bed. He lay down beside her, propping himself on one elbow to gaze down at her. She had a sloppy grin on a face surrounded by a halo of auburn hair so dark it was almost black. He reached out to trace a tattoo along her stomach to where it cupped the underside of her breast, eliciting a satisfied shiver.

"You look smug."

He suppressed a giggle, but he knew his pride betrayed him anyway. "I do?"

She tried to frown, but it didn't hold. "Yes. Insufferably so."

In a sing-song voice, he teased, "You squirted."

"Did not."

"Yep. You did."

"Oh, shit. I'm sorry," she responded with a slightly panicked gleam in her eyes.

"*Sorry?* Why?"

"I've never done it before."

Joel felt his grin get even wider. "Awesome," he breathed.

"Oh, great. Now you're going to get a big head."

"Too late. I already have one," he quipped, glancing downward to indicate his tumescent tent.

Mona rolled her eyes. "Ugh." Even as she grunted her disapproval, one hand slithered over to grasp him through his pants. "Mmm," she purred. "Yes, you do."

"Should I..."

"Shut up and kiss me."

Joel did as instructed, guided downward by Mona's strong hands pulling his face to hers. Soft lips met his, warm and inviting. He hummed deep in his throat to express his contentment.

She pushed him back slightly and ran her tongue along his chin and lips. "Mmm, you taste like me."

"Have you tasted yourself before?"

Mona's sneer expressed her opinion of the quality of his question, but she answered anyway. "Of course I have. Have *you?*"

"Tasted you? Yes, you're delicious."

"No, dumbass. Have you tasted yourself?"

Joel faltered, his mind sorting through options before deciding on honesty. "Yes. I was curious one time. Didn't really like it."

"Huh." Mona winked at him. "Eat more fruit. It'll improve the taste."

"I don't..." Joel felt flummoxed as his mind tried to find a response.

She smacked him lightly on the chest, although lightly for an orc still caused him to grunt. "Improve the taste for your partner, you selfish dipshit."

"Right, sorry." Joel shook his head. "My mind is catching up, because I do care about your pleasure."

"Did I actually squirt?"

Back on solid conversational ground, he responded with enthusiasm and delight, "You certainly did. I felt it splash on my chin."

Mona's eyes widened. "It wasn't gross?"

"No, not at all. I loved it."

"There's your smug smile again."

"Sorry. No one ever squirted on me before."

Mona rolled her eyes. "You're incorrigible. Shut up and kiss me again."

Joel nuzzled into her neck, nipping and kissing. He kept at it as she squirmed and moaned. Her skin was smooth and warm under his lips. Saltiness teased his tongue as he licked his way to her jagged earlobe. His light nips provoked a deep whine from Mona's throat.

"Is this okay?"

"Don't fucking stop, Joel."

He did as instructed. She twitched and twisted under his tender ministrations, filling his ears with her joyful clamor. He clamped down with his teeth and yanked softly on her earlobe and ran his tongue along the series of golden rings on the lower edge of her lobe. Each soft keen from Mona sent a pleasant tingle down his spine.

"I need you to stop," she demanded in a husky voice.

Joel backed off before grunting in surprise when Mona rolled him onto his back. She held him down with one hand pressed firmly against his chest, kissing him with desperate passion. With her other hand, she fumbled with the waistband of his pants. He arched his hips and assisted her as she slid his pants down. The garment stuck briefly on his stiff rod before smacking his pelvis with a 'thwop' once freed. Together they managed to slide his pants off.

Once he was naked, Mona threw her leg over Joel, straddling his waist. He quavered when her hand grasped his cock. She rubbed his lower head against her dewy lips. Joel mewled with desire as Mona leaned down to kiss him.

Their tongues danced a sensual tango as she slowly engulfed him inside her torrid twat. He traced his fingertips down her flanks to rest his palms on her hips. Hard muscles tensed and flexed underneath his touch. Those same flexes he felt under his hands also constricted his cock like the embrace of the world's most pleasurable python.

He savored the feeling of her weight on top of him and their skin pressed together. Their closeness and connection filled him with a soothing feeling of contentment like a steaming cup of tea on a cold day. They stayed joined and unmoving for a time before Mona rotated her hips, causing him to partially slide out of her slick embrace.

Planting both hands on his chest, she lifted up onto her knees, fully impaling herself on him again. Mona began a slow rhythm, building momentum as she rode him. Mewls and moans filled the air as their bodies slapped together. He held onto her waist as her tits bounced frustratingly out of reach. Whatever disappointment he had about not being able to get his hands on her magnificent mounds dissipated rapidly under the building pressure in his groin.

Taking one hand off her waist, Joel slipped his thumb between their jackhammering bodies to caress Mona's clit. His touch seemed to light a fuse in her core as she sped up further. Up and down she rode, driving them ever closer to their impending explosions.

Joel's eyes rolled back in his head, and his muscles stiffened as he came, firing a seemingly endless supply of semen into her sodden depths. As his own orgasm faded, Mona dug her hands into his chest as her back arched and toes curled. Her fangs glistened in the light as she threw her head back and yowled out her climax.

As she came down, she collapsed onto his chest, and his arms wrapped around her. Soft lips found his mouth for a slow, comforting kiss. Mona pulled the curtain of her sweat-slicked hair off his face and tucked it behind her ear. He stroked her hair and back while she laid her head on his shoulder.

"You did so good, Mona," he murmured. "Thank you."

She responded with a weary head nod and a quiet, "Uh huh."

Chapter 11

Stargazer

Rainbow

There was a damp spot under Joel's ass when he woke up. He found himself spooned against Mona's back with his arm draped across her and a firm boob cupped in his hand. Her chest rose and fell with each gentle snore, and he could smell hints of wood smoke, vanilla, and sweat in her hair.

I vaguely remember falling asleep with her still on top of me. She must have rolled off in the night. Her skin feels amazing. I wish I could stay like this forever, but I need to pee badly.

He slowly disentangled himself from Mona, provoking a hitch in her snoring and a dissatisfied grunt. Frozen in place, he waited until her snoring resumed before sliding out of bed. Picking up his chilly pajama pants from the floor, he threw them on and padded downstairs. He added tinder and a couple logs to the stove before stirring the embers. By the time the tinder ignited the solid blocks, his own morning wood subsided enough to make urination possible.

Once done in the bathroom, he pondered the possibility of breakfast and what he might fix for himself that would not wake the sleeping orc. He craned his head around when he heard a footstep on the stairs. Mona paused her descent halfway to let loose a toothy yawn. Joel gawked at her naked body underneath her unbound bathrobe.

"Morning," she acknowledged him breezily. "Thank you for getting the stove going. The heat feels good."

It took a second for her greeting to penetrate the miasma of lust enshrouding his mind. "Oh, right. Good morning to you, too."

"Joel, are you all right?"

He could feel hot blood coursing into his cheeks and ears. "Yeah. I'm great." He realized he was staring, but he couldn't stop. "Fantastic, actually."

She giggled and glanced down before asking, "Should I cover up?"

"Um, no. Yes? Whatever you feel most comfortable doing is fine with me. I don't have a preference or anything."

Ignore my last lie and please don't cover up. You are beautiful beyond words, and I wish I could tell you instead of babbling like a fool.

Joel continued babbling, "Because it's entirely up to you, and I don't want you to feel like you should do what I want, and—"

Mona grabbed the lapels of her robe and opened it wide while crooking one leg to expose her cum-encrusted pussy and upper thighs. "You came inside me a *lot* last night."

"Um." Joel wasn't certain what the correct response should be, so he feebly ventured, "Sorry?"

She chuckled in response. "I'm not upset about it. Actually, I'm a bit flattered. Do you want a closer look before I pee and clean up?"

His feet drew him inexorably closer as his head nodded. He stopped at the stairs and ogled her as she squatted in front of him.

"You're so gorgeous and sexy," he murmured.

Long green fingers cupped his chin and drew his gaze from the lewd display between her thighs up to her glittering amethyst eyes.

"Good boy," she purred. "Now what are you making me for breakfast?"

Her compliment sent a thrill rocketing through his mind. "Eggs and sausage?"

"Perfect." She gave him a pat on the cheek before she rose and sashayed the rest of the way to the bathroom. He watched her go, knowing she knew he was staring at her.

Once she was out of sight, he returned to the kitchenette and prepared breakfast. They sat down together at the table, and Mona kept her robe open.

"I have to ask. Why are you giving me a show?"

She smirked at him. "Because teasing you is fun. Also, the sex last night was fantastic, and maybe I'm hoping for an encore before we leave."

"I see. What if I'm not interested in a quickie?"

Her fork came to a sudden halt halfway between her plate and her mouth. "I'm sorry. *What the fuck* did you just say to me? Are you seriously not interested?"

Joel leaned forward. "Oh, I am *extremely* interested. My attraction to you is rock solid right now. The thing is: I don't want to fuck you again. I want to make love to you."

"You're shitting me."

He grimaced. "I assure you, I am not." Joel reached across the small table to wrap his fingers around Mona's hand, hoping she didn't stab him with the other. "I want to stop avoiding this conversation with you."

"Why?" Irritation seeped into her voice. "What is so important about talking about something which will never happen?"

Joel's frustration finally shattered the walls in his mind and freed his feelings from their prison. "Because I love you, Mona. You were my first love, and no one else has ever measured up to you. Now, after all my fuck-ups, maybe I want to take a chance and truly love the most magnificent person I've ever met."

She stared at him in stunned silence before slowly lowering her fork to her plate. A moment later, she raised it back to her mouth and ate. He waited patiently as she finished her breakfast.

In a weary tone, she finally grunted, "Fuck off, Joel."

"No," he shot back forcefully.

"What?"

"You heard me. Mona, how do you feel about me?"

Her eyes narrowed as she leaned back in her chair.

Before she could open her mouth, he added, "Please be honest."

Mona's expression oscillated between a frown and a grimace while she carefully considered her next words. "My feelings don't matter, because this can never work between us. You'll never stay, and I refuse to let you break my heart twice."

"How are you so certain?"

"Because I'm an orc, Joel. We don't have citizenship. We don't have status. We don't have rights. This country has elected, *twice,* an asshole who wants to deport us all. Where? Fuck if I know. The portals that brought orcs here were destroyed forty years ago, and our world was dying even then. Even if the portals were rebuilt, there might not be a planet to send us back to. Right now, the plan is to ship us off to any country that will take us, even if they happen to be a failed state embroiled in an endless civil war." Her eyes narrowed as her fists clenched. "Because we're not people to these motherfuckers. We're subhuman trash to him and his millions of supporters despite all we do for this ungrateful fucking country."

"There's no way—"

"You don't know," she spat. "He might, or he may just decide to find another solution. Something shall we say...final."

"The American people would never stand for it."

She glared at him with narrow eyes and protruding fangs before she threw her back and laughter rang out, cold and mocking. "You want to bet on the *kindness* and *decency* of the average human? More specifically, would you bet *my* life on it?"

Joel collapsed against the back of his chair. He wanted desperately to affirm the common decency of his fellow citizens, but he knew he'd be lying. "No," he breathed. "If anything, human history is littered with the horrors we've often gleefully inflicted on other humans. Anything is possible, especially when it comes to orcs."

"As I'm sure you're aware, we can't become citizens, and our children are also denied citizenship, even if one parent is human or elven. Some states are even bringing back one-drop laws and anti-miscegenation laws, just for orcs."

"I know."

"Do you, Joel? You might grasp all this on an intellectual level, but can you truly understand what it means to be deemed an 'other' your whole life? To struggle to find work because businesses would rather hire humans? Or the businesses which are willing to hire orcs pay us less and provide little or no benefits. It's harder to get loans or higher education simply because we're orcs. Can you imagine a fucking lifetime of the same bullshit, over and over?"

He remained uncomfortably silent as his brain tried to process.

Mona let her fangs out as she spit her fury. "We're branded as inherently criminal, even though our opportunities are constrained by society, often leaving us with fewer choices for legitimate work and even fewer choices for legitimate work which also pays enough to cover rent, food, transportation, and the shitty excuse for health care in this country. They call us 'lazy,' yet at the same time we're also supposedly stealing jobs from 'real Americans'—which is simply code for humans—and I say just humans because no elf would stoop so low as to compete for a job with an orc."

She stabbed the air with her fork for emphasis. "All of this is nothing but bullshit used by the elites to pit working class humans against orcs for their own power. They give humans someone to hate, someone to look down on, while they rob them blind."

"I've heard those arguments before."

"It doesn't make them less true. You've done fine for yourself, even if your life has experienced setbacks. Now, why don't you take some time and review all the turning points in your personal history. Just think about each of those inflection points and how the course of your life might have gone differently if you had fangs and green skin."

Mona stood up and closed her robe before stalking over to drop wearily into her chair. She was soon joined by Itsabella. Meanwhile, Joel was lost in his thoughts.

Would Ed have given me a job if I'd been an orc? Definitely not. He trained me, and I took over his business when he had his heart attack. He never had a kind word about an orc. Or most humans either. Okay, Ed was racist to the core, but I shut my mouth, nodded along, and did my job because it benefitted me. The business did better once he was dead because I was willing to work with orcs and the sorts of humans Ed wouldn't. One of the slogans I've seen on protest signs is "Silence is complicity." Every time I didn't speak up, I was helping myself, but at what cost to my soul?

Then there was high school, when my parents bullied me into ditching Mona. I was silent then, too. Why? Because it benefitted me. I traded love for college. What a shitty deal.

Would Cheri have married me if I were an orc? Definitely not. I could have dodged a bullet if I had been. Probably not something to bring up with Mona, though.

Joel watched Mona scratch and coo at Itsabella, who was draped across her chest. Her book sat abandoned on the small table beside her. The orc and the cat cuddled until Itsabella decided it was time to get down and curl up in Mona's lap. Mona stared off into nothingness as Joel returned to his own thoughts.

I've worked hard all my life to get where I am, even if where I am in life isn't great right now. Did I get any special breaks for being human? No, not really. On the flip side, being human never worked against me either. I remember when Coach Evans told Ruprecht he wasn't smart enough to be the quarterback. Ruprecht was way smarter than Tommy, and we might have won a couple of games if he'd been quarterback, but Tommy was human. Coach gave some racist bullshit about orcs not being capable of leading a team. Did I say anything? No, of course not.

In school, at work, it's the same shit. I remember the orc carpenter on the Alta Vista job in Scottsdale saying something about the poor quality of the materials. He got fired, and the whole building collapsed a week after opening. The owners tried to blame the workers, but the investigation found them liable for using substandard materials. The more I think about it, the orcs were often the best workers on most job sites, yet they always got the shittiest pay and worst tasks. Fuck.

Okay, so what am I going to do about this? A few things, I guess.

Joel stood up and refilled their coffee mugs. He walked over to Mona and placed their mugs on the small table beside her before taking a seat on the ottoman.

"May I?" He asked, placing his hands on her feet.

"A foot rub?"

"Yeah. While we talk."

She scratched Itsabella's head, murmuring softly to the cat. He waited until she lifted her head to look at him. "We can talk. You can rub my feet so long as it doesn't disturb this little creature."

Itsabella purred loudly in response, her low rumbling providing a counterpoint to the crackling logs inside the wood stove.

He worked his thumbs into the sole of one foot before speaking. "Thank you for talking with me. I feel like opening up how you did was probably painful, so I want you to know I appreciate your sharing with me. You gave me some deep subjects to contemplate."

"And what are you thinking?" She asked with a wary tone.

"My head is somewhat jumbled, and I'm sure more will come out as I process things. One important theme I've noticed and which needs to change is my own silence. Too often I've shut my mouth because opening it wouldn't benefit me, or worse, because it was easier."

"Explain, please."

"I feel worse because at least if there is a beneficial reason, then I can excuse it with selfishness. If I'm silent simply because it's convenient, then what does that say about me?"

Mona snorted derisively. "Honestly, nothing good, whether it was for selfishness or because it was the easy road."

"You're right. I don't want to be a coward anymore." Joel halted his speech and hands at the same time. Mona poked him with an insistent toe. "Sorry," he mumbled as he resumed rubbing her feet.

"What's on your mind?" she asked.

Joel's shoulders slumped as he sighed. "I guess I'm thinking of some guys I ran into a lot in college and on job sites. They're all very much into being 'real men.' Their definition of what it truly means to be a man mostly seemed to mean being an asshole. They were dismissive of women, kindness, orcs, and a whole host of other subjects. I feel like the younger version of me looked up to guys like these as role models of masculinity, but they weren't. They're just douchebags."

"No shit," Mona scoffed.

"Not even just assholes. They are fragile and afraid…" Joel stopped kneading again as he sought the right words. Mona poked him with a toe, and he continued the foot massage. "It's like everything about them was a performance. A grand façade to hide their own insecurities. Now I feel even worse for not having the strength to speak up back then. I took the easy path because I felt that standing up for what is right was hard."

He broke eye contact with her as his shame nearly overwhelmed him.

She flexed her toes on one of his fingers, causing him to cease studying the floor and look up at her. "Yeah, it is difficult. Empathy and kindness take strength and courage. Cruelty and hatred are the refuge of cowards." Mona smiled at him, and it felt warm and genuine. "Congratulations on achieving a new level of enlightenment, but what are you going to *do* now?"

"First, I pledge to stand up for what's right and not be silent anymore."

"Ooh." Mona's smile ran away. She shrugged and wiggled her fingers before her expression slipped into a scowl. "Talk is cheap, Joel."

She's right. Bravery is simple when there's nothing on the line. I'm not sure how I can prove my commitment to her, but just as importantly, I need to demonstrate my resolve to myself. I'll figure it out, somehow.

"You're right. Which applies to the next bit as well. I'm starting a new business in Portland. Master electricians can always find work, and I'm sure there are opportunities to be had. As I grow my business, I'm going to bring on orcs, pay them a good wage, and treat them well. I can't undo past mistakes, but I can be better."

"Uh-huh." Mona didn't look convinced.

"There's one other thing I thought of."

"Hmm?"

"Mona," he said softly. "Come to my parents' place for Christmas dinner—as my date."

The shock on her face is exquisitely delightful.

"Abso-fucking-lutely not," she hissed through clenched teeth.

Chapter 12

Heroes

David Bowie

How dare he? After everything I told him. What is possibly going through his mind? Is this some kind of trick, or has the sex addled his mind? Great, I fucked him stupid. I can't think of any other explanation for why he would be this idiotic.

Joel dug his thumbs into the sole of her foot as he spoke. "Is this because of high school? I'm very sorry for how I hurt you. I was a coward, and I was wrong. If I could do it all again, I would have stood by you."

"So, is this you angling for a do-over? Your chance at redemption?"

Let's see how he spins this. He's clearly thinking of a clever response.

He nodded his head and gave a tiny shoulder shrug. "Kind of, yeah. I screwed up badly, so I want a second chance to do right by you."

Mona couldn't keep the edge of surprise out of her voice. "I wasn't expecting honesty."

"I'm not done," Joel responded as his eyes widened in alarm. "I mean, I'm not done with being honest. I wasn't lying when I said I love you or how no one has ever measured up to you. You told me again and again how *we* can never work. I hear you, and I believe you're wrong."

The small hairs on the back of her neck stiffened, and she felt her heartbeat increasing. With an effort, she stifled her anger and replied in a carefully measured tone, "I would *love* to hear why you think I'm wrong."

"There's a connection here. Not just the sex—which is mind-melting, by the way. Reading with you, talking, cooking meals for each other." The corners of his mouth twitched upward, accompanied by a giddy gleam in his eyes. "It feels amazing and special. Tell me you don't feel it, too."

"It doesn't matter, Joel. None of this does. We're snowed in at your cabin, so we're making the best of it. This isn't the real world. How long does your special feeling last when we're holding hands walking down a street and people are staring at us? Or when your parents and friends ask when you'll stop going green and get married again to a human? You know—when reality drops on your head like a ton of bricks."

"You didn't say you didn't feel the same thing," he replied with a happy smirk.

Mona threw her hands in the air, provoking an alarmed squawk from Itsabella. "Great Goddess, did you listen to nothing I just said?"

"I heard you describe a hostile outside world where prejudice and bigotry will negatively impact our relationship. Also, I noted your concern around my resolve, which I sadly submit is well-founded."

Mona snorted, inciting another irritated glower from the cat.

"Tell me honestly you don't feel something."

Fucking asshole. Why does he have to be so insistent? Yes, he's taken good care of me when I was injured and otherwise hasn't been awful.

"Again, my feelings don't matter."

He smiled triumphantly like a kid who got an extra slice of birthday cake. "So, you do have feelings for me."

"Fuckin' A, Joel. I can't have feelings for you. You're my best friend's brother, and you already broke my heart once."

"For which I am eternally sorry. I will spend the rest of my life making it up to you."

"Ugh," Mona snorted. Itsabella stood and shook out her fur in a huff at this latest disturbance. She stalked down Mona's leg and curled up in Joel's lap.

Joel's lips turned down into a small frown. "You're right, you know."

"I am?" Mona was confused by the sudden switch.

"We're going to figure out how to break this to Tiffany, especially in light of her wanting to have sex with you." Joel flashed a toothy grin. "I hope my sister isn't jealous."

"Why would—Joel, what the hell are you talking about?"

"My apologies. I was trying to lighten the mood a bit."

"You…"

Goddess, I know I'm not good about prayer and everything. Probably something about not being sure if you're real since we're on a different planet and our old world was dying anyway. Sorry. I'm getting distracted. Any divine guidance here? Do I trust my treacherous heart and accept this ridiculous overture or listen to a decade and a half of brutal experience telling me this is the insipid inspiration of an imbecile?

Mona waited for a divine response.

Anything?

Fuck.

Joel waited patiently for her, resting his forearms on top of Itsabella as he continued to rub her feet. The satisfying sensations from his fingers and knuckles radiated up her legs.

"Stop rubbing my feet."

He paused immediately.

"Oh, fuck it. Keep massaging my feet."

A brief cloud of concern crossed his visage, but he resumed his ministrations as instructed. He still said nothing.

"Let's suppose I consider your ludicrous suggestion. What then?"

He flashed her his teeth before schooling his face into a subdued expression. His gleefully glimmering eyes betrayed him, though.

"Obviously, my invitation to Christmas at my parents' place still stands. If you'd rather not, then we could go on a date sometime soon. Um, I still need to find a place to stay in the meantime, but we'll figure something out."

"Yeah, where *are* you staying?"

"I was hoping to crash with Tiff for a couple days while I find a place."

Mona snorted. "Not a chance. Flora doesn't allow men to stay over."

"Flora?"

"The elven bitch she rents from. She's a stuck-up assgoblin who thinks having a male in the house will turn the place into a brothel. Honestly, a whorehouse would be an improvement, but that's just one orc's opinion."

"Wow," Joel snickered. "You don't like this Flora person."

"No, not in the least. Want to guess the one thing she hates worse than having men in her house?"

"Orcs?"

"Look at you, figuring it out in one guess."

"I'm catching on quickly."

"You could stay with me."

What.

The.

Fuck.

Why did I say such an absurd thing? Has the sex made me *lose my mind? I should say something else while he's still stunned.*

"Thank you for the kind offer. Are you sure?"

No, I am absolutely not sure. Actually, I am one hundred percent certain of my own mental incompetence. Now is my chance to say it was a mistake.

"Yes, stay with me."

Is there something wrong with my mouth? What am I doing?

"Mona, I would stand up and kiss you, but Itsabella is so comfy in my lap."

She smiled as she shrugged. "I will accept your reasoning." She stretched out a toe to scratch the cat under her fuzzy chin. "Also, can I tell you how much I enjoy your adoption of Itsabella's true name?"

He chuckled. "It suits her. I'm still going to call her Bitsy as well."

"Me, too."

"Seriously, though. I can't tell you how much I appreciate you giving me a place to stay. I swear it will just be for a day or two until I can figure something out. You're absolutely certain about this?"

The dam containing Mona's inner monologue burst, and her brain dumped its contents in her mouth. "*No.* I have no idea why I offered to let you stay with me. The idea is preposterous, and yet now I can't stop thinking about it. I'm supposed to be deciding about my future and my life, but instead I'm thinking how convenient it would be to have you around to bang whenever I'm in the mood."

"I should decline, then. You need your space."

"But—"

"Anyway, being your readily accessible flesh dildo isn't what I'm looking for," Joel interjected.

She felt her eyebrows arch. "Seriously?"

A delectable shiver tingled her spine when his visage faded into a determined frown. "I'm not playing around, Mona. Turning down the best sex of my life isn't a decision I would make lightly, but you mean more to me than just a readily available piece of ass."

Intense Joel is kind of sexy. When was the last time anyone looked at me with the same kind of stubborn determination? Well, plenty of entitled men who think groping a stripper is their God-given right have given me a similar look before I beat their asses. In this particular case, it's endearing. There's a subtle flush in his neck and ears, and he's breathing slightly harder. I think he means what he's saying, at least for now. Regardless, his stare is getting me wet.

"Stay with me. Just for a couple days."

"You're sure?"

"Yes, dummy," she retorted with an exasperated sigh. "We'll do Christmas with your parents and reassess afterward."

He's cute when he's pleasantly surprised. I wonder if he would have the same expression if I popped a butt plug into his ass?

Mona lost herself in a fit of giggles, startling both Joel and Itsabella.

"What's so funny?"

"Just the look on your face." *The look of someone surprised by a butt plug...*

A tear sprang from Mona's eye and streaked down her cheek as her laughter redoubled. Joel frowned as he tentatively probed his face with a finger, eliciting another gale of guffaws from the giddy orc.

"It's not *that* funny."

"Oh, it is. You have no idea."

He crossed his arms in a pout. Itsabella stood in his lap and bonked his limbs with her head, demanding the resumption of scratchings. With a grunt, he complied, his glower fading as the magic of cats mellowed him out.

She resumed the conversation, saying, "I still need to figure my life out."

"Would it help to talk about it?"

"Shouldn't we be shoveling snow or something?"

"We can if you want. I know you were hoping to leave today."

Mona felt a twinge in her gut as she recalled her vitriolic tone yesterday. "Maybe we should listen to the weather forecast. If it's good, then I would like to stay another day." Before he finished opening his mouth to respond, she added, "With you."

He gently lifted a protesting Itsabella and handed her to Mona. "Here you go." Bitsy started massaging Mona's lap while Joel strode over to the radio.

"He does have a nice ass, doesn't he?" she whispered to the cat.

Joel called out, "Did you say something?"

"Nope."

"Okay. Radio's on. We should have a forecast at some point. I think our coffee's gone cold. Do you want something to drink? Water? Tea? I can make another pot of coffee."

"Tea would be lovely, thank you."

"Coming right up."

She rested her chin on one palm while she observed Joel puttering about the kitchenette. He hummed along to the music as he filled a teapot and prepared two mugs.

"What did you think, little girl? Am I out of my mind for hoping he and I could work out?"

Itsabella responded with a rumbling purr.

"I know. Everything I've ever experienced reinforces just how catastrophic this idea is, but somehow I keep wishing it will be different this time. Oh right, doing the same thing over and over again is the definition of insanity. Do you ever feel this way?"

Bitsy uncurled her head, then settled her chin on her forepaws with a quiet huff.

"You're not helping."

The cat's ears rotated toward Joel when the teapot shrieked, then back to Mona.

"Thank you for listening."

Itsabella isn't helpful, but watching Joel is entertaining. He's kind of hot, despite the stupid comb-over, and how do I say 'no' to a shirtless man who massages my feet and makes me tea? I don't, apparently. I invited him to stay in my apartment, because sure...why not.

"Here's your tea." Joel handed her a mug before sitting on the ottoman again.

"Thanks."

"Snow this afternoon at higher elevations but light rain for us. We'll need to get out tomorrow, though, or we won't get home before New Year's Eve."

"Sounds good."

"Do you want to talk about your life plans now?"

Mona's heart beat faster, and her skin suddenly felt clammy. "We don't have to. It's not a big deal."

He leaned forward and grasped her free hand with his. "Come on. I told you my plans and hopes for the future. Tell me what you're thinking."

"No. You're going to laugh at me."

"I promise I won't." His mouth pinched into a contemplative moue. "Well, I guess it depends on the idea, but I'll try not to."

She rolled her eyes at him. "You suck."

He stared at her with an insipid grin on his face.

"*Fine,*" she snarled. "I want to open up a frozen yogurt shop. Or ice cream. Probably both, actually."

"Fuck, yes," Joel gasped. "I love locally made ice cream. Are you going to make basic flavors like vanilla and chocolate, or will it all be artisanal flavors?"

Mona couldn't contain a hearty chuckle. "Slow your roll there, dude."

"Sorry. I have a weakness for ice cream, and I got excited."

"I can tell."

His face colored as he glanced at his tummy. "Hey. I know I'm not ripped like most guys you probably date."

"First, I wasn't commenting on your stomach. Second, most of the guys—and gals—I've dated didn't have six packs. It's not on my must-have list."

Joel looked somewhat mollified. "Good, because I'm just being frugal."

"Frugal?"

"Yeah. Instead of having six abs, I just have one." He stared at her expectantly after he delivered the punchline.

"Your jokes are terrible, but I appreciate the effort."

He pouted at her.

"Oh, don't give me your sad face."

The pout ran away, replaced by a wry smile. "You're right. It was not my best joke. I promise to do better in the future."

She snickered. "Yes, I expect better from you. Although I have extremely low expectations for boyfriend jokes."

Boyfriend? By the looks of it, he's as shocked as I am. Is my mouth just doing things on its own now? Is my subconscious sabotaging me? What is going on today?

"Well, I guess I'll just have to up my game so I can earn the title," he responded with bravado. "You clearly deserve better quality humor."

She nodded her head as regally as she could manage with a lap cat and a mug of tea. "Obviously. I'm a lady, you know."

"You are."

Affecting a stern countenance, she attempted to steer the conversation back to reality. "Enough fooling around. Do you like my ice cream and FroYo shop idea?"

"I love it," he exclaimed. "You'll have some fierce competition, but I feel like there's space in the city for you. What's stopping you?"

The whole world. Or at least it feels like it most days.

"Well, for one, I have no idea how to run a business. Also, I'm an orc, which means getting a loan is going to be somewhere between difficult to impossible. I can get a loan from other orcs, but those are usually attached to organized crime, which I prefer to avoid.

Then there's finding a suitable location—again a process made more difficult due to my green skin."

"Are you venting, or do you want problem solving?"

She chortled. "You've had experience with this."

"Let's just say the reason I'm divorced wasn't me."

"I'd like to hear more about your divorce and why you're here later."

"Do we have to?"

"You had to suffer through me venting, so I might as well return the favor." After he rolled his eyes at her, she continued. "For now, if you have any solutions, I'd love to hear them."

"If you can't get a bank loan, then I can lend you money."

Danger. Danger. Don't mix money and feelings.

"I'm not taking charity."

"Nor am I giving it. It would be a loan. I'd charge market rates on interest. Alternatively, I could be an investment partner in your business. Having a human on board might make things easier with the bank."

The hairs on the back of Mona's neck bristled and her fangs popped out. "Fuck off, Joel. I can do this on my own."

He reached out for her hand again. "Mona," he said in a gentle, soothing tone. "You just gave me three logical reasons why you *might not* be able to do this alone. How about this? Give it a shot on your own. If you want help or advice for dealing with bankers or realtors, then I'm happy to help. If you get shot down, then let me help you. I absolutely understand why you have your heart set on succeeding on your own terms, and I overstepped. I'm sorry."

Her neck hairs slowly stood down. "Apology accepted. I appreciate your eagerness to assist me. I would like to get some strategies for dealing with these people."

"Absolutely. I want to help as much as I can." His accompanying smile was warm and gentle. "Would you prefer to talk more closer to time?"

"Yes, please." She sat back, waiting patiently.

Let's see if he says something stupid again.

"I wish you the best, Mona. I think this is a phenomenal idea, and I can't wait to try your ice cream and FroYo. I'm not sure if I like FroYo."

"What?"

"The word, not the thing. What's wrong with calling it frozen yogurt? Do we have to shorten everything?"

"Would you like to yell at the kids on your lawn, too?"

Joel's face turned beet red before he laughed. "Fine. I deserved that."

"Yes, you did." Mona coughed and felt her own cheeks warming. "Since you've offered, I can think of one thing you could do to help me."

"Of course. What is it?"

"If I find a space to rent, can you check it out to see if it needs work? I assume I'm going to get ripped off."

Joel's answering grin was feral. "I would *love* to. Maybe I can even get some business out of it if the wiring isn't good enough."

"You are quite the entrepreneur."

"Small business owners have to hustle. You'll find out soon enough."

She cocked an eyebrow at him. "Do you honestly think so? I'm not out of my mind for trying to open a frozen treat shop?"

"Mona, you're brave, smart, and capable. I believe in you."

"You haven't seen me for half my life. Why are you so sure?"

"Because, you were the same way in high school and even middle and elementary school. Yes, you've changed since then. I'll admit some level of ignorance there, but you don't have to trust my word for it. Trust hers." He nodded to Itsabella.

"Trust the cat?"

"Yes. She hated Cheri and clearly loves and trusts you. Honestly, little Bitsy is a much better judge of character than me, so I choose to follow the wisdom of my favorite feline."

By his logic, should I trust Itsabella's opinion of him? Possibly. My own judgment hasn't been spectacular over the years, so maybe I should also trust the cat. Could Itsabella have steered me any worse than my own heart and mind? No. Well, if I'm going to trust one pussy, then I might as well trust two.

"Joel, do you want to read for a bit until Itsabella gets up, then fuck me silly again?"

"Yes, but only if you'll settle for making love to me."

Chapter 13

Love Again

Dua Lipa

H er eye roll was adorable. "Fine. In the meantime, pull up a chair and read with us. Obviously, Itsabella isn't reading, but you know what I mean. I can't believe I agreed to Christmas with your parents."

And I can't believe I asked her. This is going to be a disaster. At least Tiffany will be there, so it will be three against two. Unless Tiffany is upset with me because she has a thing for Mona. Shit. I'll need to talk with Tiff as soon as I have cell service again. I hope she's cool.

Joel pulled his chair next to Mona's before asking, "Hey, can I borrow another book? I finished the first one."

"Go for it."

"Thanks, I'll be right back, and this time I won't touch your dildo."

The pointed tips of her ears darkened, and the small tufts of hair at those points bristled, but she laughed instead of lambasting him. "Unless you want to borrow it."

"Where would I..." Joel figured out where the dildo would fit. "Thanks, but I think I'll pass."

"Suit yourself." She chuckled at his discomfort. "Before you go, I've been meaning to ask you about the decor."

"What about it?"

Mona gestured at the flower print window dressings and the vintage logging tools on the walls. "Did you all have a designer?"

Joel chuckled. "Cheri wanted a designer. She envisioned Swiss chalet chic. Unfortunately for her, I'd already built the place before we married and had it decorated with some cool antiques."

Mona eyed the two-person wood saw above the doorway in skeptical silence.

"Okay, I might have made some questionable choices, but there's some cool stuff in here. The dining table, for instance."

"I do like the big axe." Mona glared at him. "And do *not* make a comment about orcs and axes if you want sex again."

"Nope, not saying anything."

"What about the straight razor in the bathroom?"

"Yeah, that one is me, too."

Mona popped an eyebrow up. "Ever used it?"

Joel shook his head. "I've never had the guts to do it."

"Hmm."

"Cheri did get some things, though. The window dressings..."

"What about these chairs?"

Joel chortled. "Oh hell no. Cheri wanted these fancy, stiff, super elegant chairs that wreck your back."

"Good call on the veto, then." Mona chuckled, then turned to her book. "Go get yourself a book."

He trotted upstairs to grab a book from her collection before returning to situate himself next to her. Setting his bare feet next to hers on the ottoman, he reached into Mona's lap to pet the cat. With his other hand, he propped the book open and started reading.

It wasn't long before he felt Mona's toes nudge his foot on the ottoman. Peeking over, he could see her still engrossed in her book—seemingly oblivious to the innocuous contact happening at their lower extremities. Taking his cue from her, he continued reading but pressed back. They stayed like this for what seemed like hours, but based on what little Joel managed to read was only minutes. He found his concentration slipping as he ran his toes up the sole of her foot. Another stolen glance revealed her still nose deep in her book even as their toes parried and thrust.

Any pretense Joel had of reading shattered when she laid a hand on Itsabella's back, partially covering his. "Are you actually reading?" He asked as her fingers entwined with his, sinking into Bitsy's soft fur.

"Obviously. What else would I be doing?"

She can't possibly be unaware of our feet and hands. Sure, her tone sounds innocent, but it must be an act.

Mona continued, "Aren't you reading?"

"I'm trying. I keep getting distracted."

"Hmpf," she sniffed. "I'm not sure what would distract you up here in this lonely cabin."

She's definitely messing with my head now. There! I see a little smile. She knows what she's doing, the temptress. Two can play this game.

"You're right."

He was able to read some more, even as he was conscious of their connected hands and feet. After some time, their mutual touches became less titillating and more comfortable. Eventually, he lifted his head from his book and turned to gaze at her.

Somehow she is even more breathtakingly beautiful each time I see her.

Seemingly sensing his stare, she glanced over and blinked at him. "What?"

"I appreciate spending time with you. This feels good—not just good. Perfect."

"I'm not sure I'd go as far as perfect, but yeah..." She paused and sighed. "I'm enjoying spending quiet time with you."

"Sorry, did I make you uncomfortable?"

"No. I'm good, but thank you for asking." Mona let slip a satisfied purr. "I'm surprised just how relaxed this feels." She squeezed his hand. "We should do this more often."

He felt his eyebrows crawl up his forehead. *I like the sound of "we."*

"I agree. Maybe when we get to Portland, we can carve out some time for ourselves." He snickered before adding, "You know, when you aren't using me as your own personal sex toy."

Mona guffawed, startling her lap cat. "Oh, I'm sorry, little lady." Unmollified, Itsabella stalked across the adjacent chair arms over to Joel's lap and settled into a ball. "See what you did, Joel? I lost my furry lap warmer."

He couldn't contain a snicker. "My evil plan worked."

"Not cool, Joel. Not cool," she complained with a shake of her head, but he ascertained the faintest hint of a smile on her lips.

"My bad."

Looking from her amethyst eyes to the emerald skin of her hand ruffling Itsabella's fur, he giggled. He placed his own hand on hers, jointly stroking the gently purring cat.

She stuck her tongue out at him but didn't move her hand. Instead she returned to her book. After observing her for a bit, he did the same.

He finished four chapters when he felt a squeeze on his hand. Returning the squeeze, he swung his head around to meet Mona's luscious lilac gaze.

"Hey," he whispered.

"Hey."

"Are you having a good day?"

She rolled her eyes toward the ceiling thoughtfully. "Yes, but it could be better." Mona flashed him a lusty wink and a toothy grin.

He responded with a sly, "Is there anything I can do to improve your day?"

"I can think of a few things..." Mona uncurled from her chair with the sinuous grace of a prowling leopard. She tucked her hair into a messy bun before pulling the cushion from her chair. The cushion landed on the floor with a soft smack underneath Joel's outstretched legs.

Her grin was feral and hungry as she placed both hands on his legs and jerked them off the ottoman. His feet slapped on the ground and Itsabella bolted from his lap in an affronted leap. Her fingertips swaggered up his thighs to his waist.

"May I?"

Joel struggled to form words or even coherent thoughts, but he did manage to arch his hips. Fingernails scraped his skin as Mona hooked her long, jade fingers into his waistband and yanked his pants down. The cabin air felt cool on his still flaccid cock, although the blood rushing from his mostly useless brain was at least heading somewhere productive.

Mona's tongue tip traced her lips hungrily as her eyes feasted on the twitching meat in his lap. She pulled her shirt over her head and knelt on the cushion.

"You...don't have to," he stammered.

"Shut up, Joel. I'm about to ruin you for other women."

He gasped when she touched him, her fingers and palm warm on his skin. His heartbeat thundered in his ears as she slowly stroked him to firmness. Once he was fully hard, Mona ran her tongue from the base to the tip, then down to trace the rim of his aching helmet.

She winked at him before she enveloped him with her lips. He moaned as she sucked him deeper inside her hot and humid mouth. The flanks of her fangs rubbed against his phallus as she bobbed her head. One hand stroked him in time with the movement of her mouth, sending electric sparkles shooting across his sputtering brain.

Joel groaned as she withdrew her mouth from him. She gazed at him with glittering violet irises and a wicked grin. Mona queried him in a sibilant, throaty tone, "Are you ready?"

He barely managed to reply hopefully, "Ready for more?" before she silently opened her mouth again. The sharp point of her fang subtly pressed against the hyper-sensitive head of his cock before she inched him inside her open orifice again. Millimeter by millimeter, her fang caressed his tender flesh along its journey.

The feeling of the sharp tooth sent waves of terror crashing through his blood, mixed with extreme ecstasy. Whatever rational part of his brain which was still functional screamed about the potential for permanent damage to his vital organ and his amygdala fully concurred, but his pulsating pleasure centers overrode caution and fear.

Mona ran her tongue along his cock as she slowly and steadily worked deeper inside. The combined danger and delight quickly overwhelmed Joel's endurance.

"I'm...Mona...Oh, no...Mona," he gasped, but she only flicked her eyes up to meet his own briefly before his eyelids snapped shut, and his cock pulsed rope after rope of cum into her expectant throat.

Oh, fuck. Oh, fuck. Oh, fuck. Am I still alive? If I'm dead, then at least I died happy.

Reality returned when Mona slurped the remaining cum off of him and swallowed audibly. His dick felt suddenly cold, and her hands pressed into his thighs as she pushed herself up. Behind still closed eyelids, Joel waited for whatever would come next. Finger-nails slid up his heaving chest to rest on his shoulders. Strong palms gripped him as one knee slid into the space between his waist and the soft side of the chair, then the other mirrored on the other side. Lips pressed against his mouth, and an insistent tongue probed for entrance.

His eyes fluttered open to find Mona's exultant visage hovering in front of him. He opened his mouth, and his tongue met hers in a slow tango. The salty taste of himself lingered in her mouth, but Joel was beyond caring about such trivialities. He twitched when her moist, meaty, honeydew-green lower lips caressed his still rigid rod.

"Oh, fuck," he murmured as she sank down on his staff.

She purred, "No, dear. We're making love."

"This isn't how I pictured it."

"Funny," Mona responded with a grin. "This is *exactly* how *I* envisioned it. Okay, maybe not the chair."

Joel's beleaguered brain couldn't come up with a verbal response, so he simply elected to say nothing. He found himself fascinated by the contrast between his Arizona-enhanced tan and her viridian coloration as his fingers meandered across her smooth, warm skin. They found one of her tattoos and began to trace the black ink. His hands skipped when Mona slid upward on his steel-hard cock.

The warm air of the cabin still felt cool compared to the cozy confines of her cunt. More of him was exposed to the air as she gradually lifted up until they were barely connected. Joel whimpered at the possibility of separation, then sighed when Mona steadily sat down again, once more encasing him in her tight, silken grip.

He slumped down in the chair to give her more room to move while he gripped her hips to assist the unhurried rhythm of their love-making.

Mona's tongue and fangs skimmed the sensitive skin of his neck, summoning shivers as he angled his head to give her better access. She worked her way up to his ear, where she hummed and moaned as she nibbled.

His hands lifted in response, snaking their way to her bouncing breasts. He fondled and cupped them in his palms while he pinched and rolled her nipples between his fingers. Mona drew a ragged breath and nipped lightly at his ear before murmuring, "I love what you're doing, but I need something different at this moment."

Joel wistfully slipped his hands to her sides, then to her back. Arching his fingers, he dragged his short fingernails down Mona's back. The gleeful groan in his ear encouraged him to retrace his way up her back at an agonizingly languid pace. She undulated underneath his fingertips, sending a fresh wave of sensations crashing through their enjoined genitals.

"Oh, fuck Joel. Feel free to never stop."

"You like it?"

"Mmm-hmm," Mona purred into his neck.

He traced his hands back down to her taut ass before ascending her spine all the way to her skull. Unknotting her bun allowed him to massage her head as her hair fell across his face and chest in a silken curtain.

One strong green hand pressed against his chest, while the other tucked hair behind her ears as she straightened up. His own hands fell to her upper arms, feeling the coiled cables of her biceps.

"Did I do something wrong?"

"No, babe. You were great, but if you kept it up, then I might have gotten *too* relaxed. I don't want to fall asleep during sex."

"I'm pretty sure I'd die of embarrassment if you did."

"Me being so relaxed is kind of a good thing."

"I hadn't looked at it that way." Joel felt a surge of shame, but decided he needed to be honest. "Um, I probably won't be able to cum, but I want to make sure you do."

Mona snickered softly. "The blow job was too much for you?"

"It was unbelievable. Honestly, I'm not sure how I'm still hard afterwards."

She silently increased her pace, cavorting up and down like he was her personal Pogo stick. Mona flashed him a wicked smirk. "You are as solid as marble, and I'm not going to take it for granite."

"I...can't...believe...you...made...a pun...during...sex," he stuttered between bounces. Her succulent softness around his shaft and enthusiastic use of his lap as a trampoline was robbing him of coherent thought.

Mona eased off and leaned in to kiss him. "Have you ever been with an orc before?"

"Besides you? No."

"We have many skills. Mmm, so many skills."

"I'm going to have to take your word for it."

"You don't believe me?" She came to a sudden halt.

"Oh, I definitely believe you," he responded in a panic. "I just want to limit my sample size to one very special orc."

"Good answer." Mona resumed pistoning in his lap. "You better not be saying that because I'm currently impaled on your cock."

In response, he cupped her chin in his hands to draw her in for a lingering kiss. Her amethyst eyes glittered within the obsidian halo of hair framing their faces. A shiver ran down his spine when his tongue found her fangs and triggered the memory of the ecstasy she'd brought to him only a short time ago.

Mona altered her rhythm, pausing to grind her mons into him at the end of every down stroke. Strong fingers dug into his chest as she drew back from their kiss. Her hot breath huffed in his face, and her fangs glistened in the light.

Guttural grunts filled his ears as Mona's rhythm rapidly devolved. They both whined as her fingers dug into his flesh.

"Cum for me, Mona. You've got this."

"Uh huh," she whimpered.

Joel slipped a hand down to coddle her clit, and his touch on her button set off an explosion. Mona's back arched as she jerked wildly in his lap. He held on for dear life until her ecstatic convulsions ground to a halt. She collapsed on his chest, and he held her there with her head resting on his shoulder. A shiver ran through her torso when he ran his fingernails down her sweaty back.

"Too much," she murmured.

"Sorry." He placed one hand on her back while the other gently stroked her hair.

"It's okay. Thank you for holding me."

"I'm happy to."

"Why do I feel like I can fall asleep in your arms so often?"

Joel couldn't help the jovial tone in his response, "Because we have so much astounding sex?"

She smacked him lightly on the arm, although it left a bit of a sting on his bicep. "You're an idiot, even if you're probably right."

"Honestly, I'm both flattered and delighted to know you feel comfortable falling asleep with me."

Mona scoffed. "You should thank whatever god or gods are applicable I'm even speaking with you—don't mention fucking you."

"Oh, I am truly thankful, and I believe this time we were making love."

"How are you such a romantic?" She punctuated her question by nuzzling his neck.

"I wish I knew. Maybe it's because I believe I've finally found true love."

The only answer to his statement was a gentle snore.

Chapter 14

Big Balls
AC/DC

*W*hy does the bed feel so weird? And why am I cramping? Oh, shit. I fell asleep on top of Joel, and we're still both buck naked. This is embarrassing. Or is it? He probably loves having me fall asleep on him. By the feel of it, at least part of him is pleased by this arrangement.

"Sorry about going to sleep. Are you okay?"

"Not gonna lie, I'm feeling a bit..." His face flushed adorably.

"I'm getting heavy, aren't I?"

"I mean, I wouldn't say it in exactly those words, but yes."

"You could have moved me, you silly oaf."

"Maybe." His expression softened as he continued, "But you looked so peaceful. I didn't want to disturb you."

"So instead you poked me awake with your stiff friend down there."

Panic filled his eyes. "Oh, gosh. I didn't mean to. He just has a mind of his own sometimes."

"Shh, I'm teasing you. Your trouser snake didn't wake me, although he feels rather solid at the moment."

"We could put him to good use if you want," Joel suggested hopefully.

"Little Joel is going to need to take a rain check. I need to stand up before my legs cramp."

"Little Joel?" She could see a pink flush bloom on his jawline.

Mona groaned as blood rushed into her legs. She staggered and gripped the chair for balance. Alternating legs, she shook life back into her aching limbs. In between shakes, she rolled her eyes at him. "Oh, hush. I'm not saying he's small, just smaller than you and only slightly less intelligent."

"*Hey.* I'm much smarter than my dick."

"Uh huh." Her tone conveyed her doubt.

"Whatever," he intoned dismissively. "Anyway, at least you're saying my dick isn't small."

She couldn't contain the snort before it escaped. Mona followed her involuntary outburst by adding, "I mean, it's a good size. On the high side of average, I guess."

"Average?" he croaked.

"Oh, sweetie. Not everyone is hung like a porn star. You do very well with what you've got."

"Huh." Joel was definitely pouting.

Ah, the fragile male ego.

"Would it help if I told you it was the biggest I've ever had?" Mona asked sweetly.

"Only if it's the truth."

"Okay, I guess not." She reached over to cup his chin. "I don't care if you're not the biggest guy I've been with. What matters is getting the job done. And Joel..." She paused for effect. "You are *definitely* getting me where I need to be."

"Thanks."

"Oh, quit pouting. We're having amazing sex." She squatted down to feed more wood into the stove before walking over to a window. "As much as I enjoy hanging out with you while we're both completely naked, let's go shovel some snow."

"The forecast said rain was coming, which should help melt some of it."

"It will also make the snow heavy as hell, so unless you want to shovel extra tons tomorrow, let's get some snow cleared."

Joel acquiesced to her superior logic and heaved himself out of his chair. She watched him ascend the stairs.

Naked isn't a bad look for him. He needs some tattoos, though. And some time in the gym. He's got some nice muscles in there, but he needs some definition. His ass is great, though. Not a bad looking cock, either—as far as those go.

She followed him upstairs to get dressed.

He whistled appreciatively. "Are you sure you don't want to—"

"*Joel,* we're shoveling snow. If you're good, then I might reward you with some pussy later."

Great Goddess. He's like a puppy with a new treat. He better not think he can trade me in for a new one, although after the blow job earlier, I'm pretty sure he's hooked for life.

As if he were psychic, Joel commented, "About earlier…I've never been able to stay hard like I did." His cheeks and ears flushed scarlet. "You know. Right after cumming so hard."

"I told you. Orcs have secrets."

"What are some other ones?"

She flashed him a glare in response.

"Right. Got it. Secrets. Forget what I asked."

"See, you are smarter than your schlong."

"Ew, really? Schlong?"

"What? You don't like AC/DC's 'You Shook Me All Night Schlong,' or Linda Ronstadt's 'Schlong, Schlong Time,' or—"

"Please stop," he cried.

"Sorry. What's wrong with…that word?"

He threw his hands in the air. "I don't know. Nothing, I guess. It's just weird coming from you."

She scoffed. "Please. How many euphemisms do you have for *penis*?"

Joel tapped his foot and tried not to look her in the eye. "A lot."

"But it's somehow strange if *I* say it?"

"No. I'm just being stupid."

Mona giggled. "We can agree on that."

He rolled his eyes at her. "I'm never going to be able to listen to AC/DC the same way again."

Her giggles morphed into full-on belly laughs.

"What's so funny?"

"*Dude,* have you ever actually *listened* to AC/DC?"

"Of course, I'm a big fan."

She laughed at him. "Half of the Bon Scott-era songs were neck deep in double entendres."

He shot her a look of righteous indignation before his expression collapsed and he muttered, "You're right. The Brian Johnson era didn't have quite the same way with words, did it? I mean, they had some great songs, but Bon took twisting a phrase into an art."

And who says men can't be trained. Well, some of them. There are plenty who are beyond help. I have hope for this one. Hope. It's been a long time since I felt it. About fifteen years ago when we did this the first time. A good reminder to keep a leash on my feelings.

"Come on. Quit stalling, and let's go shovel some snow."

They cleared snow until their arms and backs ached and sweat ran down their foreheads. By the time they finished, they'd taken the top layer off most of the road, although they would still likely have some heavy shoveling ahead the next day.

Back at the cabin, they stripped off their coats and pants. Mona eyed Joel as he stood next to the stove in just his underwear and a loose t-shirt. The fluffy Maine Coon rubbed herself against his ankles in a frenzied display of feline affection. Her human squatted down to pet the cat, cooing softly to her.

One more night of whatever this escape from reality has been. I might as well take advantage of it—and him. Hope might be too great a leap for me, but maybe I can allow the tiny sliver of a chance of a relationship between us working out. Itsabella better not steer me wrong.

"I think she missed you."

He craned his head around to look at her. "I'm pretty sure she missed both of us. She likes you a lot."

"And you said she didn't like Cheryl?"

"Cheri, not Cheryl, and yeah—Bitsy and Cheri tolerated each other at first. I think Itsabella sensed something was wrong when she started cheating on me."

Mona arched an eyebrow at the fluffy Maine Coon. "You must have the world's smartest cat."

"Like I said, she has a sense for people." Joel shrugged. "At this point, I trust her judgment over my own."

"What happened with you and your ex anyway? I remember Tiff going to your wedding. Was it three years ago?"

"Four, actually. A buddy and I went out one night to some honky-tonk bar in Phoenix. He told me there were always some hot chicks—um, women—there in the mood for dancing and some-times more. Turns out, he was right. Anyway, I ended up dancing with this cute blonde for most of the night. We had some drinks and chatted when we needed a break from dancing. I could have left it at a one-night stand, which in retrospect would have been the better choice, but instead we exchanged numbers. We met again for dinner at one of those upscale restaurants where everything is super fancy and the portion size is about three bites. I hated it, she loved it, which again, should have been a warning sign."

"But you got sucked in by the lure of the blonde."

Joel let loose a deep, shuddering sigh. "Yep."

"After years of watching guys empty their bank accounts for strippers, I can assure you that you aren't the first, and you won't be the last guy to follow his penis into doom." She shrugged. "I've also seen it go the other way, too."

"I can see why you're so guarded about our future, among many other reasons."

"Yeah, no shit," Mona said, shaking her head. "So, what was a woman with champagne tastes doing in a honky-tonk in the first place?"

"Cheri worked in marketing, so she and some colleagues were there supposedly for research purposes, but mostly to blow off steam after a difficult project. Anyway, as much as I was blinded by the blonde hair, perfect makeup and manicure, and her classy clothes, she apparently was tired of dating cookie cutter white-collar douchebags."

"So, she decided to slum it with a blue-collar douchebag instead."

Joel frowned at her remark but then shrugged his shoulders. "Yeah, considering our history, I deserve that. I was the different kind of guy she thought she was looking for. At least I was right then. Dating Cheri was fun and exciting, and eventually, I proposed. The first year or so of marriage was good. We got to travel and try new things. Then, she got a great job offer at a new firm. She'd be a project leader there, with a huge bump in salary."

"And you didn't want her to take it?"

His eyes widened in shock. "No, I encouraged her to take the job. I'm not an asshole."

"I have a different recollection," Mona rumbled.

"I'd like to think I've learned and grown a lot since high school, or I'm trying to. Anyway, Cheri took the new job, and suddenly things were different. She was working longer days and on the weekends sometimes. I felt like I was all alone most of the time, but I kept telling myself it would be worth it in the end because once she settled in and established herself, then things would go back to normal."

"I guess not."

"Nope," he sighed. "About a year or so ago, Cheri started talking about having a kid. I didn't like the idea because she was working so much, so we fought about that a lot. I wanted to wait, but Cheri disagreed. She even told me since I made less money I could quit my job to raise the kid."

Mona snickered.

"Yeah, I know. A lot of guys say the same thing to their wives, and you're enjoying the role reversal. You're not wrong. It's a shitty thing to say, no matter which partner says it." Joel sighed. "You're not really partners if there's not mutual respect."

She nodded. "Yep."

"I'm not sure if she was already fucking her boss by then, but I guess after I balked on the idea of us having a kid, she was definitely fucking him. Marc—her boss and the guy who owned the company—was also married at the time."

"Oh, shit. What a bitch."

"*Bitch* seems like a mild term, but I agree. Of course, he was just as culpable, and just as much of a bitch. Anyway, she finally wore me down on the pregnancy thing, so we came up here in August to…you know."

"*Ew.* In the same bed we've been sleeping in?" Mona shuddered. "Gross."

Joel gave her an apologetic look. "And the hot tub."

"What the hell? *Really?*" Mona mimed retching. "I've been naked in the hot tub, and you two fucked in there. I'm gonna be sick."

"Oh, please. You can't realistically come to a secluded mountain cabin and expect that *no one* has ever had sex there, can you?"

"No, but it's still disgusting to think about."

"Our sex has been disgusting?"

"It's different."

"I don't see how."

In a forceful tone that would have made her freshman English teacher proud, Mona responded, "Joel, trust me, it is."

"Sure," he said, clearly unconvinced. "Anyway, I'm pretty sure she already had a bun in the oven and was just trying to make me think it was mine. Everything went to shit at their company Halloween party when Marc's wife caught them fucking in his office."

Mona winced. "Ouch."

Joel's eyebrows rose. "Right. How stupid do you have to be to have sex during a company party?"

"Stupid or arrogant. Either one is applicable."

"Marc is nothing if not arrogant."

"In my experience, most men are."

Along with being fragile and overly emotional, but Goddess forbid you ever call them out on either of those things. There's nothing I hate more than hearing men complain about how women are too emotional for leadership when centuries of evidence proves otherwise. As much as I loathe elves, at least they are generally smart enough to allow their women to run the show.

Joel frowned again. "Again, ouch."

See, emotionally fragile.

"Sorry, do go on about your ex and her boss."

"After the Halloween debacle, Cheri told me she was in love with Marc and having their child. Then she demanded a divorce, which I was very happy to give her."

"Is Marc divorcing his wife as well?"

"Cheri said he was in love with her and divorcing his wife so they could be together."

"Sounds like a match made in Hell."

He snorted. "Truth."

"I'm sure they'll be very happy until a younger blonde comes along and catches his eye."

"I hadn't thought of that."

She silently raised an eyebrow in disbelief.

Joel grinned with a slightly madcap gleam in his eye. "Okay, fine. I've been thinking about it a lot, and plan to savor the *schaden-freude*."

"Good."

"Seriously? No women's solidarity or anything?"

Mona scoffed and shook her head. "I've seen a ton of people like Marc. If he cheated on one wife with her, then he's definitely going to cheat on her. She probably knows this but thinks somehow she'll be the exception."

"Cheri always had a high opinion of herself."

"Somehow this doesn't surprise me." She laid a hand on Joel's arm. "Thank you for telling me. I know it wasn't easy."

"You're welcome." His expression lit up expectantly. "Any relationship disasters you want to tell me about?"

She smirked at him. "Nope. I've never been engaged, much less married. Just the standard mix of shitty boyfriends and unserious girlfriends."

"How many women have you dated?"

"You're thinking of a threesome, aren't you?"

"*No.*"

"Uh-huh."

He gave her his best innocent look. "I'm just curious, nothing more."

"Fine. I've had four girlfriends, two of whom were strippers. The longest I ever dated anyone of any gender was seven months."

"Have you ever had a threesome?"

"*I knew it,*" Mona exclaimed.

"You brought it up," Joel retorted, skin flushing pink from neck to ear. "Now I'm curious."

"Sure. Just curious." Mona felt her fangs popping as she frowned. "Twice. You know my seven month relationship? The first threesome was supposedly a birthday present from my boyfriend at the time, but a week later, he ended up leaving me for the other guy."

Joel winced. "Ouch."

"I know, right? Honestly, I'm just happy Dean is able to live his truth."

"What about the second time?"

"As you might expect, I was skeptical about threesomes after my first experience. The second one was also a birthday present, but this time for Tiffany's boyfriend at the time."

He pointed an accusatory finger at her. "Hang on, you said you've never slept with my sister."

"We've slept together a lot, platonically. As for having sex with your sister, this doesn't count."

"How do you figure?"

"We both had sex with…Tony? Ben?" Mona waved her hand dismissively. "Whatever his name was. Anyway, we both had sex with her boyfriend, and in between the two of us messed around a bit, but it wasn't anything serious."

"Like making out?" His face and neck were getting a bit red again.

Mona threw her arms over his shoulders and around his neck to pull him nose-to-nose. She could feel the burgeoning bulge in his underwear pressed against her mons. "Yes. We did some kissing and heavy petting, but we didn't go down on each other or anything." She mashed her nose against his. "Also, are you getting hard thinking of your sister?"

"*No,*" Joel exclaimed. "I'm hard because I'm thinking of you."

"With other guys?"

"Mona, come on. No, you're beautiful and sexy, and we're talking about sex. Okay, sure. A threesome sounds fun, but not with another dude and *definitely* not with my sister, and only if *you* wanted it."

"*I knew it,*" Mona exclaimed. "You can't stop thinking of three-somes."

"Okay, I'll admit you're right." He held up his thumb and fore-finger. "I thought about it a little bit."

"And I'm smarter than you."

He snorted. "Thanks for stating the obvious."

"We're good?"

"Yes, we are. Mostly. Except now I'm thinking of you and my sister and another dude, and I just want the imagery to go away."

Mona pressed her lips to Joel's and slipped her tongue into his mouth as she ground her rapidly moistening mound against his cock.

"Better?" She asked as she pulled away slightly.

"Much, although now I have another problem."

"Is it a *big* problem? Maybe your thinking is too *rigid?*"

"Large and calcified, like a stalagmite. Or is it stalactite? I can never remember which is the top and which is the bottom."

"I definitely prefer being the top, but sometimes I like the bot-tom."

She could feel a developing damp spot in her panties, and Joel felt incredibly solid against her abdomen.

"I've noticed you enjoy being on top. I don't mind at all."

"Good boy," she purred. She lightly nudged him backward. "But now, there's something I want to do, if you're willing."

"Does it involve sex?" Joel asked hopefully.

Mona reached over into his thinning hair and ruffled his comb-over. "No. It's this."

Joel's expression fell. "Oh. Is it that obvious?"

"Sweetie, yes. But I have an idea."

"I'm scared."

Mona giggled. "You should be. You know what they say about lemons and lemonade? Do you trust me?"

Joel didn't hesitate for an instant. "Completely."

Interesting. Time to see how sincere he is.

"Then get me the straight razor and vintage shaving kit from the bathroom and then go take a shower. The barber scissors, too."

"Oh shit."

"You can say 'no' if you want."

He shook his head. "No, let's do this."

While Joel was in the shower, Mona got to work. She heated water on the stove and threw a damp towel in the fridge. The razor blade was dull, but a whetstone among the antiques soon gave it a wicked edge.

Joel looked nervous when he came out of the bathroom. Mona patted a chair, inviting him to sit.

"Why is there a whiskey bottle next to the chair? Have you been drinking?" he squeaked.

Mona chuckled. "The booze is for you. Don't worry, I am perfectly sober."

"Okay, good." Joel exhaled a huge sigh as he sat down. He pounded a shot, followed quickly by a second one. "I'm ready. I think. Are you sure you know what you're doing?"

"Yes. I went through my own bald phase a few years ago, so I've been on the receiving end of this quite a few times."

"I feel better now. What's first?"

She picked up the scissors. "I'm going to trim you down as close as I can. This is your last chance to get out of this."

Joel took a deep breath and blew it out loudly. "Let's do this."

"All right." Mona gripped a hank of Joel's hair between her fingers and snipped it off. She repeated this process again and again until he was as closely shorn as she could get it. "Are you good?" she asked.

"Yeah. I'm looking forward to this."

"Trust me, you'll love the next part." She grabbed a warm bottle of massage oil from over by the wood stove and squirted some in her hand. Joel oohed and aahed as she massaged his head. "Feel good?"

"Amazing," he moaned.

After she'd fully massaged his head, she thoroughly wiped her hands, then ran over to the kitchen and poured hot water into a deep bowl, which she brought back to the work station. Mona took the antique boar bristle brush and dipped it into the hot water before applying it to the soap dish. The soap inside was yellow and cracked, but lathered up quickly from the brush and water.

"Wait here." Mona dipped a towel into the hot water on the stove with a pair of tongs and waved it in the air until she could touch it without scalding herself. She wrung it out, thankful for tough orc nerves before bringing it over to Joel. "Tell me if this is too much," she said before wrapping the towel around his head.

"Oh, that's..." Joel stiffened, then relaxed. "Mmm. A bit warm at first, but it feels pretty good now." He moaned again when she began kneading his shoulders.

Once he was loose, Mona peeled the cooled towel off his head.

Goddess, thank you if you're listening. Now keep an eye on me for the hard part, because he apparently trusts me.

Mona covered Joel's head in another good coating of foamy lather before she rinsed off the brush and picked up the razor.

"If I drank four shots of whiskey, that counts as sober, right?"

"*What?*" Joel exclaimed.

"I'm teasing you. Are you ready?"

"Not cool, Mona. Not cool."

She giggled and set the blade to his skin at the back crown of his skull. With a steady and firm hand, she drew the razor forward in a short stroke from the back to the front, clearing a small strip through the lather.

"Shh. I've got you. You're too rigid. I'm very sorry about my joke."

"Okay, I'll try to relax."

"Think of lazy weekend mornings making love in the sunlight," Mona purred.

"Wow, I…"

Mona brought the razor to the crown of his skull again, but he was still too tense.

She climbed into the chair, straddling his lap. "Good thing you bought these big ass chairs. Is this better?"

"Yes, but, you know what would be even better?"

"Fine," Mona grumped, but just for show. "Would you prefer it if I shaved you while topless?" She was already reaching for the hem of her shirt because she knew the answer.

"Yes, please."

Mona grinned to herself inside her shirt as she pulled it over her head. Her sports bra followed quickly. "Better?"

"Mmm hmm."

This time, Joel wasn't quivering with worry, and the blade skated across his skin with a satisfying "shick." Again and again she gingerly scraped the blade forward, slicing off long thin hanks of hair and exposing more of his scalp. Mona leaned in close, examining her movements with care. She savored the smell of the soap, the sound of the blade, and the gleam of freshly exposed skin.

Once she cleared the top, she ran her hands over Joel's skull, feeling the stubble remaining. Taking the blade in hand once more, she reversed direction. One hand steadied Joel's head while the other skated the blade in long careful arcs. Each pass of the razor elicited a satisfied hum.

"Are you enjoying the shave or the view?"

Joel groaned. "The shave is incredible, but nothing beats the view."

She ran a hand over his freshly shaved scalp. The first pass had removed the long hairs and the second pass left it smooth as an egg. "Oh, Joel. This feels—" A tongue flicked her nipple, derailing her train of thought. "Okay, that felt amazing, too, but you need to stop. I still have more to shave."

Mona picked up her razor and shaved from the top down, starting at Joel's temples and moving backward. He whimpered in disappointment when she clambered off his lap to saunter behind him for the back of his skull. With a few determined strokes, she removed the final masses of hair from his head. Once more, she reversed direction, using long careful strokes to remove any stubble left behind.

As she slid the razor across the back of his head, she heard Joel humming quietly and noticed his shoulders slump. Each movement of the blade evoked a happy noise, and she had to keep his head steady as his neck loosened.

"Joel, are you falling asleep?"

"No, I'm just very relaxed, which seems kind of strange to say when someone has a sharp blade pressed to my head, but this is all very soothing. Also, I trust you completely."

"Wow. Not what I expected." Satisfied with her work at the back, Mona walked around and plopped herself in Joel's lap again, much to his delight. "I'm almost done." She dipped the blade in the water, knocked it clean, then pressed to his temple and slid it along his skin. Joel's breath tickled across her breasts as he moaned. She felt wetness pooling between her thighs as her nipples pebbled. Each time her razor slid across Joel's skin, he groaned his pleasure onto her, and her own arousal increased.

Mona felt a surge of disappointment when the razor made its final pass. "Wait right here." She reluctantly climbed off of Joel's lap, glancing at the hungry erection tenting his underwear as she did. Mona cleaned off the razor, then walked to the refrigerator to retrieve the final towel.

Joel shivered when she wrapped it around his head like a turban. She rubbed him down, cleaning off any remaining soap and debris. "How does it look?"

"Goddess, Joel, I've never had a thing for bald guys, but *damn.*"

"So, it's good?" he asked hopefully.

Mona insinuated herself into his lap again. "Mmm. It makes me want to polish *both* of your heads." She wiggled her butt against his hard cock.

"Um, okay. Any time."

Her stomach rumbled loudly. Mona gave him a quick kiss on the lips and hopped off of his lap. "I need you to stop attempting to seduce me." She licked her lips. "I'm hungry, and what's in your boxer briefs isn't enough to satisfy me right now."

"You think I'm trying to seduce *you*?" Joel spluttered. "You've been grinding yourself on me, and—"

"I think we have enough chili left for both of us," she said merrily, ignoring his wagging jaw as she strode toward the kitchenette. "Finishing the leftovers means one less thing to worry about tomorrow." She mixed the leftover chili and rice together and placed the bowl in the microwave. Once the food started reheating, she pulled off her remaining underwear to pose fully nude in front of Joel.

"Let's eat naked like some decadent French royalty."

He snapped his slack jaw shut before answering. "Did they actually eat with no clothes on?"

"I feel like I read something about one of the Louis and his mistress, but I could be wrong."

"Seems likely. Kings were weird."

"Monarchy as a concept is freaking strange."

Joel considered her statement as he dropped his boxer briefs. "Yeah. You're right."

"You don't think eating naked is too odd, do you?"

"Yes, but I'm willing to try it. If I didn't, then you'd probably put clothes on, and I prefer seeing you like this."

Mona raised her eyebrows and her voice. "Oh, so you want me perpetually unclothed?"

He raised his hands defensively. "I'd say situationally starkers. I like you in clothes, and I'm looking forward to seeing you all dressed up sometime."

"*Really?* Do tell," she retorted, not bothering to hide the sarcasm.

"You're stunningly beautiful, Mona. I'd love to see you in a fancy cocktail dress at some gala or just a night on the town."

"I guess I'm just your arm candy now."

Joel snarled and stomped his foot. "Damn it, Mona. Can you just fucking stop being an asshole for a minute?"

This should be good.

"Okay, fine. One minute."

"Ugh." He clenched his fists as a frown wrinkled his face before his expression smoothed out. "You're not some plaything for me. I'm serious about us. Do I want to show off by having the smartest, funniest, drop-dead sexiest woman in the world next to me? Yeah. Absolutely."

Joel stepped up until he was arm's length from her. "Mona, I'd be the luckiest man alive. The key thing for me are the words 'next to.' I want to be your partner—in everything. You aren't some gaudy bauble—and you sure as hell aren't trash, either. You've been hurt before, and I can't ever fully understand your experiences, but I'm trying. You have every right to be distrustful about humans in general and me in particular, but I plan to spend the rest of my life proving myself worthy of your trust. And your love."

Aw. He looks so earnest and cute. Maybe I have been giving him too much shit. Unless he's a master gaslighter, at which point I'll have to kick his ass. I really hope he's not an asshole.

"I'm sorry for teasing you." She added with a grin, "And when I find the world's smartest, funniest, drop-dead sexiest woman, I'll be sure to punch her in the face."

He rolled his eyes. "I meant you."

Mona sashayed up until she was nose to nose with Joel, delighting in the barely restrained lust in his gaze. "I know." She reached out to run her fingernails from his jawline down his neck and around his nipples all the way to his belly button. Her hands hovered there briefly before descending further to cup his rapidly engorging erection. "And don't you *ever* forget it."

"I won't. I can't."

"Good boy. Now let's eat and then make love again. I'll even allow you to be on top this time."

Chapter 15

Ridin' The Storm Out
REO Speedwagon

Joel woke up in the middle of the night to an insistent head bonk from Itsabella. He grumbled groggily at the cat and reached behind his head to lift the edge of the blankets. She crawled underneath, and her soft fluff trailed down his naked backside until she came to rest in the crook of his knees. He fell back asleep with a soft cat behind him and Mona's firm, smooth skin in front.

I could get used to this.

When he woke again to the sound of a slamming door, he was alone in the bed. He threw on clothes and stripped the bed, bundling the lust-stained linens into the washing machine. By the time he was done, he was greeted by an arctic blast of air as Mona hustled through the back door.

"Great Goddess' tits, it's cold out there," she exclaimed. "The hot tub is draining. I'll go out to check on it after breakfast."

Joel chuckled. "Good morning to you, too."

"Sorry. Good morning. I made coffee. Want some?"

"Can I get a kiss first?"

She made a disgusted face. "Ew. Morning breath. Brush your teeth, and *then* I'll kiss you until your toes curl."

He nodded in assent and took care of business. When he exited the bathroom, Mona fulfilled her promise before handing him a steaming mug.

"You snore, by the way," she grumbled.

"*Me?* You sound like a bear."

Her eyebrows rocketed halfway up her forehead.

"A very—I mean, *extremely*—sexy bear who I am forever grateful for because she allows me to sleep next to her."

"Better." She lifted a hand with her thumb and forefinger held barely apart. "About this much better." Mona whirled on her heel, but he could hear her mumbling, "Comparing me to a bear..."

Before he could defend himself, Itsabella rubbed herself against his ankles. "Good morning, little lady. How are you?"

Itsabella twisted around to rub herself against him again before bonking him with her head. He squatted down to scratch her, then ended up kneeling on the floor when she plopped onto her side. Bitsy rolled around giddily as he petted her.

"Aw. She loves you," Mona gushed.

Joel looked up to see Mona standing above them. "She does. She's such a wonderful cat."

"I fell in love with her fluffy highness immediately." Mona nudged him with her foot. "Egg, cheese, and sausage sandwich for breakfast?"

"Yes, thank you."

"I hope you like plant-based sausage, because that's what I eat at home."

"Wait a second. You're telling me we ate fake sausage yesterday?"

Mona giggled. "Yes. See, you can't even tell the difference." She wiggled her hips enticingly. "Now stop staring at my ass and set the table."

"How did you know?"

She twisted her head around to smirk at him. "Lucky guess."

Joel did as instructed, then fed Itsabella, finishing around the same time as Mona. "Aw, the three of us are going to eat together like a family."

Mona raised an eyebrow at Bitsy's bowl, where the last morsels were being devoured. "I like the sentiment, but neither of us eat that fast." Itsabella sat back on her haunches and stared at them expectantly. When the second breakfast didn't arrive, she began grooming herself.

After Mona and Joel finished their breakfast, they stepped into the whirlwind of packing, cleaning, and preparing the cabin to survive the rest of the winter without damage. By late morning, they were finished and standing next to their respective vehicles.

"Are you ready?"

"As I'll ever be," Mona responded.

Joel turned his car around, now facing the access road to the highway. *"I hope she'll be all right,"* he thought as he stared at the leather-clad orc on her motorcycle behind him. Feathering the gas, his car lurched forward, tires crunching on the ice-slicked snow. He kept his speed low and fingers gripped tightly to the steering wheel. The final stretch sent his heart rate into overdrive as the snow was higher here, although definitely tamped down by the rain. He was almost through when his car ground to an involuntary halt.

"Shit."

In his mirror, he observed Mona dismount from her motorcycle and walk forward. He reached for his car door but stopped when he saw her waving her hands. Instead, he rolled down his window.

"Don't try to get out. The snow is kind of deep."

"I figured."

"We knew this could happen. Give me a couple minutes."

"Okay."

Joel rolled up the window and watched Mona trudge back to her bike. She pulled a hand axe from her bag and stepped into the woods. He was watching her chop down a sapling when the weather report came on the radio. His fingers tapped impatiently on the wheel as the forecaster gave the report for the various sub-regions of northwestern Oregon.

I forgot how irritating it is to have separate forecasts for metro Portland, higher elevation Portland, the coast, the coastal mountain range, the Willamette Valley, the Columbia Gorge, Mt. Hood, the Cascades, and then the high desert. Oh, shit. We're in trouble.

He rolled down his window to holler at the orc as she dragged the sapling to the front of his car. "Mona, there's another atmospheric river coming in, meeting strong winds from the east. If we can't get out of here soon, we may need to turn around and hunker down."

"Keep your shit together. We've got this."

He took a deep breath and kept his foot off the gas as she shoved the cut sapling under his tire. When she stood up and stepped back, giving him a thumbs up sign, he gently touched the gas pedal until he felt the tire catch on the fallen tree. Gripping the wheel and increasing the gas, he inched the car along the fallen tree until he broke out of the snow bank into the area at the highway entrance they'd cleared a few days before.

A tap on the window shook Joel from his breathless reverie. He rolled it down and Mona leaned in to plant a sloppy kiss on his lips. "Good work."

"You, too."

"Thanks. Let me grab my bike and get out of here before the snow hits."

Her ass is amazing in tight leather. Okay, she's on her motorcycle. Focus on the road ahead, Joel.

"Are you ready, Itsabella? Here we go."

She answered with a plaintive cry.

"I know. We'll be at Mona's home soon. You can stretch your legs then."

They weren't on the highway long before the snow started coming down. Swirling snow devils danced along the highway, whipped up by the deadly battle between the dry, frigid air moving west toward the ocean and the comparatively warm, wet air currents flowing east off the Pacific.

His anxiety wanted out of this weather as soon as possible, but his rational mind counseled patience in the face of treacherous conditions. Joel choked down his jitters, keeping his speed moderate as they slowly descended. His heart leapt into his throat every time Mona's motorcycle disappeared behind a curtain of snow or bend in the road, followed by a sigh of relief when her headlamp reappeared.

Their pace slowed further as traffic increased the closer they got to Portland, further elevating Joel's blood pressure. He panicked when a look in the mirror revealed a car behind him instead of Mona's motorcycle. Cold relief flooded his veins when she passed him and pulled ahead. He followed her off the main highway until they reached the Killer Burger in Happy Valley.

"Come on. I need to warm my feet a bit, and we both need lunch. We'll make it fast for Bitsy's sake," she said to him after they parked.

"How much further?"

"In this shit." She indicated the snow. "Maybe an hour. Two, if we're unlucky."

After fueling up on burgers, he followed Mona into Southeast Portland. By the time they reached her place, Joel was exhausted. They pulled into the driveway of a rundown cottage and shut off their vehicles.

"Come on. Let's get Itsabella and the leftover food inside and enough stuff to get by for tonight. We'll get the rest tomorrow."

"Sure. Didn't you say you lived in an apartment?"

Mona snorted, her breath a foggy cloud whipped away into the snowstorm. "Yeah. The basement apartment."

"Oh." Joel opened the passenger door and pulled a mewling Itsabella out of the car. Mona grabbed Bitsy's gear from the back seat, and the three of them dashed for the house. Inside, they garnered curious stares from a pair of half-dressed orcs canoodling on the couch in front of a TV.

"Rook. Lex. This is Joel. Joel, meet Rook and Lex."

"Hey." They all exchanged awkward waves.

"Where's Holg?" Mona asked

"He's on night shift at the airport. Pretty sure he won't be home for a while."

"Probably not. The roads are shit right now. They'll be a nightmare soon."

The one Joel assumed was Lex asked, "How was your cabin retreat?" With a smirk, she added, "it looks like you picked up a stray."

"Joel owns said cabin and showed up unexpectedly. The cat is Itsabella. They'll be staying in the basement with me for a couple days."

Two sets of eyes widened, but Mona's housemates brought their expressions quickly back to neutral. "Cool. We can't have a human here too long or they'll raise the rent," Rook remarked.

"*Shit,*" Lex drawled. "He stays too long and pretty soon there'll be an artisanal cheese shop next door, and we'll get kicked to the curb."

The two orcs chuckled wryly, fist-bumped, then settled back to watch the television.

"Come on. Let's get Itsabella set up downstairs before we get the rest of the stuff we need for tonight," Mona said as she led him down into a dingy basement illuminated by a bare lightbulb in the ceiling. A threadbare futon rested against one wall, and a cheap particle board dresser stood against the other. "Welcome to my home shit home. Bathroom is behind the door over there. Shower is upstairs, and we have to share," she spat out tersely.

Wow. This place is incredibly depressing.

Itsabella strutted out of the carrier onto the cold concrete floor and immediately bolted for the futon.

Mona sank down into a squat to pet the cat. "I'm sorry, Princess. I know this place is a dump, but you and your human will only be here for a couple days until he finds someplace much nicer."

"I..."

Her head whipped around to glare at him. "Think carefully about what you say next, Joel."

He shrugged his shoulders. "Honestly, I've got nothing. You are strong and capable. I have no place to comment. I'll just say 'thank you' for letting us stay with you for a couple days."

Her fangs popped out of the grin spreading across her face. "You want to ride in like Richard Gere at the end of *Pretty Woman*, don't you?"

His shoulders slumped, and he loudly exhaled. "Yeah. Sorry."

She clomped over to him in her motorcycle boots and kissed him squarely on the lips. "Thank you for feeling it and not saying it. We'll see how Christmas with your parents goes, and maybe I'll even ride off into the sunset in your limo."

"For the record, I don't think you're a hooker."

Mona snorted. "Thanks, but who is hotter? Me or Julia Roberts?"

"I mean..." Joel laughed and threw up his hands in surrender when Mona glared. "I'm kidding. You're *much* hotter."

She huffed. "Ass."

"Yes, your ass is amazing, especially in leather."

Mona chuckled. "Nice recovery." She gestured toward the stairs. "Now let's go get our stuff." Joel jumped when she pinched his butt on the way up.

They hauled in food and clothes before Joel locked his vehicle. He ended up standing awkwardly behind the couch, staring at the screen while Mona stuffed food into the fridge. He asked Rook and Lex, "What are you watching?"

Lex glanced his way, and Joel tried to ignore Rook's hand sliding under her crop top, fondling her boobs. "Some cheap Christmas romcom. Rook loves these things."

"Shut up, Lex. So do you."

"Hey. I'll admit to liking them, too."

Lex shifted her gaze to him again. "So, what's up with you and Mona? You slumming it in the green?"

"It's a long story. I'm not slumming anything. I just got divorced, and she's putting me up until I find a place of my own."

"Is your ex an orc?" Lex asked. They were both examining him now.

"No. She's human. Why?"

"Just curious."

The couple on the couch watched him as he struggled for words. "Mona and I...it's complicated. But good."

Two green arms wrapped around his waist from behind. "Come on, Mr. Complicated. Let's go downstairs and leave these two love-birds alone."

Lex winked. "Don't leave on our account. Join us if you want."

"Thanks, Lex, but we've had a long drive and a longer day."

Mona led him downstairs again. They sat together on the futon, with Itsabella in between them. She asked softly, "Joel, are you okay?"

"Yes and no. I'm scared about starting my life over, but I'm excited to be here with you."

"In this shithole?"

"Anywhere with you, Mona."

"Are you serious?"

"Absolutely."

"Wait, I didn't finish the sentence. Are you seriously a complete idiot?"

Joel fell backward on the futon laughing. He sat up, wiping his eyes a short while later. "If you're involved, then my answer remains the same."

She shook her head, but he could see her lips curling upward despite her best efforts. "You're the dumbest human ever."

"I know." He waggled his eyebrows at her. "It's because you fucked me stupid. Wanna do it again?"

"Not tonight. I'm exhausted," Mona said as she heaved herself upright.

"Me too."

When Joel finished in the bathroom, he slid under the blankets on the futon and snuggled up to Mona. "Where's Itsabella?" he asked.

"By the feel of it, she's wrapped herself into a little ball behind my knees."

"Don't fart on her in the night."

"*Joel,*" Mona hissed. "Would you like to sleep in your car tonight?"

"Nope. I'm shutting up now."

Chapter 16

Coming Home

Scorpions

Mona's muscles felt tight and cramped from being sandwiched between Bitsy and Joel all night. Even so, she was warm and cozy, which was a significant improvement over most mornings in the basement. She pulled her phone from underneath her pillow and tapped out a text. Itsabella stirred when she flexed her toes, and she felt the cat slink from behind her knees all the way up her back and out. Mona rolled over just in time for a hefty head bonk. She lifted the covers to let the cat back in. The two of them shimmied until Mona's backside was pressed against Joel and Itsabella was ensconced against her stomach.

She couldn't fall back asleep, but stroking Bitsy's soft fur while Joel's morning wood hotdogged between her butt cheeks was relaxing in its own way. He mumbled something unintelligible in her ear and extended his arm over her side. His hand rested first on Itsabella before gradually shifting to cup one of her breasts. Joel snored gently in her ear while Bitsy did the same on her other side.

"Oh, shit. Sorry," Joel exclaimed when he woke up, yanking his hand back like her nipple was a hot stove.

Itsabella and Mona both grumbled at the sudden movement. Joel was saved from Mona's sharp tongue by her phone's vibration. She reached under her pillow and rolled onto her back to check her texts.

"Tiffany wants to have lunch."

Joel propped himself on his elbow, his expression alarmed. "Does she know about us?"

"Do you *want* her to know?"

There's not going to be an us if you don't. I'm not sneaking around on my best friend.

"I definitely want her to know. I'm just a bit terrified because you two had sex—"

"We didn't have sex. We just made out and stuff on her boyfriend's birthday."

"Who you had sex with." He sounded accusatory.

"At Tiffany's request, and is this really a road you want to travel down?" Mona's voice was soft as velvet but hard as steel.

He shook his head vigorously. "Nope. We both have our pasts, but the only thing that matters is our future. Together."

Maybe he's not a complete moron.

"Good answer. You may put your hand back on my tits."

Joel took her assertion as an invitation to slide his hand under her sleep shirt. Mona didn't object, especially when he began circling her nipple with soft caresses.

"Brunch in two hours over on Hawthorne work for you?"

His voice squeaked. "You want me there?"

The sensations from her breasts drew forth a quickly suppressed moan. "Did you have a plan for how to break the news to your sister?"

"Not really."

"Then why don't we tell her together."

"Sounds like a good plan." He pinched her nipple. "Whatever will we do in the meantime?"

"You seem to have something in mind."

"Mm-hmm." Joel slid her shirt up and lapped his wide tongue against a pebbled nipple. "Oh. I should brush my teeth first. Morning breath."

"Good call." Mona tapped his firm erection. "Don't lose this."

Joel hissed as his feet touched the frigid floor. He raced for the bathroom, yowling the whole way. Mona fed the cat while Joel was in the bathroom, then replaced him when he left.

Exiting the bathroom, she raced across the cold floor to the futon where Joel was waiting for her. She dove under the covers and huddled against him.

"You're naked," she exclaimed.

He flashed a lascivious smirk. "No. I'm nekkid."

"What's the difference?"

"Naked is not wearing clothes. Nekkid is not wearing clothes and wanting to get sweaty and nasty."

"*Oh.* I suppose I should get nekkid, too."

"I wouldn't object," Joel responded with a coy little smile on his lips.

"I want to warm up first."

He wagged his eyebrows at her. "It's easier to transfer body heat without clothing."

Mona chuckled. "I remember." She shucked her shirt and underwear and snuggled up against him. He felt warm, safe, and cozy, with one exception. "Little Joel is leaking on my stomach."

"Sorry. He's a bit excited."

"I bet he is." She propped herself on one elbow so she could whisper in his ear. "Want to know a secret?"

"What?"

Mona nibbled on Joel's ear, savoring his groan. "Little Joel isn't the only one who is excited," she purred.

"Now I'm the one who's leaking," Mona thought to herself almost an hour and a half later as they cleared off Joel's car. The warmer Pacific air had won out over night, shifting snow into rain which continued through the morning. The roads were a disgusting slurry of ice, snow, and water but passable. She slid into the passenger seat and glanced over at her not-quite-boyfriend. "Are you ready?"

He puffed out his cheeks before blowing out his breath. "No, but as ready as I'm going to be."

They reached their destination without too much trouble, although parking was its usual nightmare. The pair walked up to Jam on Hawthorne and put their names down for a table for three. Mona felt Joel's fingers entwine with hers as they huddled under the awning. She sighed but didn't object. The casual intimacy felt good.

"What's good here?" Joel was checking the menu on his phone.

"Everything. I like the wraps if I'm in the mood for something hearty. The French toast is great if I'm on a cheat day."

"Do you spend a lot of time at the gym?"

"This body takes work. Plus, again, I'm an orc. Most jobs for people like me involve physical activity, so I found it pays to keep in shape. No one wants to hire a bouncer who looks like they can't throw a punch."

"Sorry, I didn't mean—"

An excited voice interrupted them. "*Mona,* there you are."

They whirled to face where the voice came from.

"Who's the—*Joel?*"

"Heya, Tiff. Been a while," her brother offered weakly.

"Hi, Tiff." Mona embraced her best friend. "Look who I found at the cabin."

Mona felt her ear tufts bristle guiltily as Tiffany's gaze flicked back and forth between her and Joel. "Were you two holding hands?" her friend hissed.

"Maybe we should sit down first."

Tiffany scoffed. "No shit. I might need a stiff drink, too."

Mona swallowed nervously before exclaiming, "Mimosas it is."

"Oh, God," Tiffany's face tinged pink, then pale. "You already got something stiff from my brother, didn't you?"

Mona's silence spoke volumes.

"You dirty *slut*," Tiffany whispered with an approving smirk.

"Sorry. I didn't—"

"Hush. Are you actually sorry?"

"Only if you're upset. He's your brother after all."

"If *I'm* upset? After..." Tiffany wrapped her in an enthusiastic bear hug. "You know what? Let's get seated. I want to hear *everything*."

Once they were seated, Tiffany immediately ordered a mimosa bucket. She peered across the table at the two of them. "Okay, spill the tea. How is it you two are fucking and holding hands?" She pointed a finger at her brother. "Also, Joel, not that I ever liked the bitch, but aren't you *married* to Cheri?"

Mona chuckled, "Not anymore. It's part of the reason I took pity on him."

"It wasn't all pity sex," Joel whined.

"Whatever. One of you two needs to start at the beginning."

Mona and Joel fumbled through the tale, talking over or correcting each other at points in between sips of mimosas and mouthfuls of French toast.

"...And here we are," Mona finished.

"You dirty sluts," Tiffany giggled. "I'm so happy for you both."

Joel asked, "You're not mad?"

"Oh, I'm still plenty mad at *you* for screwing this up in the first place, then marrying the wrong woman, but at least you're finally back on the right track."

He sighed. "You know Mom and Dad are going to shit themselves."

Mona interjected, "About the divorce or you dating an orc?"

The siblings snorted simultaneously. "Both."

"Fuck 'em if they don't like it," Joel added.

"Do you mean it, Joe-Joe?"

"Wow, Tiff." Joel's voice caught, and Mona detected the glimmer of wetness in the corner of his eye. "You haven't called me Joe-Joe in forever—and yes, I mean every word."

"Good," Tiffany responded with a firm nod. "You stopped being my Joe-Joe when you broke up with Mona the first time." She pointed her knife at Joel. "So, all the stuff you're saying—I'm going to hold you to it, because Mona is my ride or die bestie. I *will* fucking gut you if you break her heart again."

Joel held his hands up in surrender. "Message received. Trust me, this is forever." He lowered his hands and leaned forward. "What about you, Tiff? What have you been up to?"

Oh shit.

Mona's hand lanced out like a striking cobra and gripped Joel's hand under the table.

Tiffany grinned wickedly at her brother. "As Mom and Dad have surely complained to you *ad nauseam*, I've been stripping since college."

"Yes, they mention it every time I talk with them."

"I'm also on OnlyFeet."

"So Mona said."

Tiffany raised her eyebrows. "Did she now?"

"In my defense, Joel had just saved my life, and my head was a bit off."

"Uh-huh. Did Mona also tell you I do some lingerie modeling and amateur porn as well?"

Joel choked on his mimosa, then hissed as Mona crushed his hand in an iron grip.

Keep your shit together, Joel. I probably should have warned you, but this isn't my story to tell. Be supportive to your sister, or I'll break your fucking fingers.

"I'm sorry, but did you say—" His voice dropped to a whisper "—porn?"

"Yes, porn," Tiffany answered as if they were discussing the weather. "Amateur, ethical, porn. Is there a problem?"

Mona held her breath.

"No. I...only want to make sure you're safe," Joel said, clearly selecting his words carefully.

Tiffany giggled. "Oh, I'm *very* safe."

"I wasn't only talking about contraception."

Her brunette friend's grin widened. "Neither was I. Every time I shoot a scene, I have someone there who prioritizes my safety."

"Who?"

"Mona."

Joel's gaze spun around to her. "You didn't think to mention anything?" he hissed.

She shrugged. "It's Tiff's life. I'm just there to support her."

"What if something—"

"*Joel,*" Tiffany's voice cracked like a whip. "Stop it. About a year ago, I was doing a scene with a new guy up from Vegas. We discussed our limits before the shoot, but when we got going, he went too far. Mona broke his arm, nose, four ribs, and his dick along with the camera guy's fingers."

"Holy shit," Joel breathed.

Mona growled, "*No one* touches my best friend without her consent. Also, the camera guy was stupid enough to come to his buddy's defense."

"How did you not get charged with assault?"

"Because it was in the contract," Tiffany answered. "I always have a clause to make sure Mona gets paid and can protect me as she sees fit. Those dumbasses either didn't read it or thought it didn't apply to them."

"So, you just beat their asses?"

Mona shrugged. "No. First, I politely asked them to respect Tiff's consent statement. Then, I angrily demanded they respect her consent. They ignored me twice. Their mistake."

"What kind of idiot ignores a pissed off orc?"

Mona and Tiffany shared a look before they answered in unison, "Horny, entitled bros."

I'm loving the look on his face. He's half terrified of me and half wanting to screw me. Men are so much fun to play with.

Tiffany reached across the table to her brother. "Are you okay?"

"Sorry. I recently learned about my bad habit of trying to be Richard Gere."

His sister looked confused, so Mona explained, "In *Pretty Woman*."

"Got it. White Knight syndrome."

"Yeah," Joel agreed sheepishly. "I'm working on this. I'll support you no matter...oh, no."

"What?"

His entire head bloomed into a brilliant shade of rose. "I'm just praying I've never watched my own sister when I..."

Mona and Tiffany burst into raucous laughter, attracting stares from around the restaurant. "Come on. It's not funny." The two friends wiping away tears disagreed but were too amused to vocalize their opinions.

Eventually, Mona gathered her wits enough to say, "I bet Joel never watches porn again." The two friends devolved into another fit of giggles.

"Not cool, y'all. Not cool."

"I'm sorry if I ruined porn for you, Joe-Joe."

"It's fine. I didn't watch much anyway. Do Mom and Dad know?"

Tiff glared at him. "No, and they better not find out."

"Your secret is safe with me."

"Moving on to non-porn topics. Tiff, do you have any ideas on where Joel could live?"

"Maybe. I forgot to ask, where's he staying now?"

"With me."

"*Mona,* damn girl. Way to go. Although I'd love to get you both out of your shithole apartment."

"Me too. But you know my problem." Mona plucked at her green skin.

"Let me think about it. There's definitely some places who will accept human tenants with orc girlfriends."

"Tiffany, you know I can't—"

"Fuck off, Mona. I have a good feeling about you two. Actually..." Tiffany pulled out her phone and tapped furiously. Joel and Mona watched her in silence, their hands casually entwined below the table. "Okay, awesome. Charity and her boyfriend are flying to Nebraska to meet her family. She says you two can crash at their place until New Year's, we just need to go get the keys right now."

"Tiff, I can't just stay at Charity's place."

"Will you stop being stubborn? She likes and trusts you. You were her favorite bouncer, and she's pissed at Gus for firing you. Plus, her place has heat, unlike your shitty basement, and you won't have to pirate the neighbor's wifi."

"Heat is nice," Joel remarked.

"What about Itsabella?"

Tiff looked to her brother. "How is she with other cats?"

"She's been an only cat for a while, but she was fine with other cats at the shelter."

"Perfect. Let me text Charity again."

Mona and Joel waited once more.

"Okay. Even better. Charity was going to have Roxy watch her cats, but Roxy's a bit flakey, so bring Itsabella over to meet Chad and Muffy. I'll text you the address. This way, so long as your cat is cool with their cats, you two can watch them, and you'll be doing Charity a huge favor. Now scoot."

"What about the check?"

"Joe-Joe, I've got it. Get out of here, and meet me at Charity's as soon as you can."

They ran for the car and hopped in. Back at Mona's, they found Bitsy curled on the futon and stuffed her into the carrier before she knew what was happening. They made it to Charity's place to find her and her looming boyfriend standing just inside the door with their luggage. Tiffany introduced them to Charity and Bruce, then they all facilitated a meeting of the cats. Chad and Muffy seemed mildly interested in Itsabella, who was mostly curious about the new space. Since there were no immediate issues, Charity ran down the care and feeding checklist with Mona and Joel before bolting for the door, thanking them profusely on the way out.

As the trio stood in silence in their temporary abode, Joel asked, "Is her name actually Charity?"

Tiffany snorted. "It's Clarissa. Charity is her stage name. Why don't you two get your stuff? I'll hang out here with the cats for a bit."

Mona and Joel spent the evening lounging with the cats and watching Christmas romcoms on the couch. The next day was Christmas Eve, and they made a run to the grocery store in the early morning for supplies. Mona took Joel to her gym and got him signed up. After their workout, the rest of the day was spent baking and decorating Christmas cookies, a process made more difficult by inquisitive cats.

He looks cute in an apron. More importantly, he looks happy. I could get used to this. Between the cabin and being back in Portland, I feel comfortable with Joel. Like we can actually beat the odds and make our relationship work.

Mona padded up behind him as he stirred a bowl of cookie batter. She slipped her arms around his waist and propped her chin on his shoulder. "Hey," she whispered in his ear.

He flicked a quick glance her way as he continued stirring. "Hiya, beautiful."

His words provoked a warm, balmy feeling in her core, spreading through her body and suffusing her emotions with a quiet joy.

"I love you, Joel."

The spoon stopped, and the bowl clattered to the table as Joel stiffened. He nudged the bowl away from the edge before spinning in her arms.

"*Seriously?* I mean, I love you, too, Mona. With my entire being. I'm sorry. I just didn't expect you to say those words, maybe not ever, and I'm so happy."

"Slow down, cowboy."

"Never." He lifted her off the ground with a grunt and kissed while spinning them around.

"Put me down, you idiot. You're going to throw your back out."

Joel reluctantly lowered her down and gently reached a hand behind to massage his lower back. "I got carried away."

Mona booped his nose with a finger. "Let me do the heavy lifting, silly boy."

"Yes, my love."

"Ooh, say it again."

"Yes, my love," he repeated.

"Those are words I can get used to hearing."

"I'm happy to whisper them to you every morning and shout them from the rooftops every night."

She chuckled. "You're an idiot." Wrapping her arms around him again, she squeezed him tight against her body. "But you're my idiot."

They stayed in their joint embrace for a minute before they heard a clatter from the table. Chad was standing there, joined immediately by Itsabella, and their noses twitched curiously toward the cookie batter.

She released Joel and bolted toward the inquisitive felines. "I'll get the cats while you go back to stirring."

They finished off the last batch of cookies and jointly fixed broccoli chicken linguine and pesto for dinner. Noshing on freshly-baked cookies, they settled onto the couch for another cheesy holiday romcom and snuggling.

Mona's phone buzzed, breaking their moment. "Tiff wants to meet us here tomorrow and take one car to your parent's place."

"Sounds good to me. What time?"

"Ten-thirty. Isn't lunch at noon?"

"Eh, more like one. My parents want us there at noon."

"Are you sure you definitely want to bring me? We both know your parents don't like orcs."

Joel snickered. "They need to get used to having you around because I love you."

"Won't they expect your wife?"

"Nah. I texted yesterday to tell them Cheri and I split. I didn't go into details over text, but they know. Tomorrow might be a bit uncomfortable, so I apologize in advance."

Mona chuckled wryly. "I figured on nothing less."

Chapter 17

Burn

Deep Purple

A knock on the door announced the arrival of Tiffany. She stood outside holding two garment bags aloft. "Hey, y'all," she announced as she strutted in with a duffel bag hanging off her back.

"What's with the baggage, sis?"

"Oh, Joe-Joe, it's a girl thing. Now go watch TV and give us some space."

Mona shrugged at him as Tiffany dragged her into the bedroom.

He flopped down on the couch and pulled up an animated series he'd been streaming in Arizona before he left. Snippets of conversation, punctuated by occasional giggles, tickled his ears, but he couldn't make out what they were saying, so he simply focused on his show.

After an hour, he started to get nervous. Fifteen minutes later, he knocked on the door to announce the need to leave, but was met by more giggling. Five minutes later, he was back. "We're going to be late."

"Mom and Dad will be fine. We'll be out in a couple minutes."

Five minutes later, he was about to knock again when the door opened, and his sister stood before him wearing a red dress with a pile of coats in her arms. "We're ready," she announced.

"Where's—" The question died in his throat as Mona emerged from the bathroom. Her nearly-black auburn hair was piled into a deliberately messy bun, leaving her face framed by two loose locks. His vision traveled down her neck to the royal purple dress draped on her shoulders. An acutely-pointed V exposed a moderate amount of cleavage. The dress hugged the curve of Mona's hips before ending just below her knees. His breath caught in his lungs when she spun around on her high heels to highlight the deep scoop of the functionally backless dress.

"Do you like it?" She asked with a coquettish gleam in her eyes.

Useless air rasped against his dry throat as Mona prowled toward him. As she drew closer, he could make out a faint hint of glitter on her chest and upper arms, sparkling against her emerald skin. One long finger reached up to tap his sagging lips.

"What? Nothing to say?" Mona's eyes danced with amusement.

"*Fuck me,*" Joel uttered breathlessly.

"Later, dear. We don't want to keep your parents waiting."

Tiffany added cheerfully, "Yes, come on, dummy. You're making us late."

"I'm—" He tried to protest, but they were already strutting toward the door. Hanging his head in defeat, he followed them feeling self-conscious about his jeans.

Joel drove them to his parents' place in Northeast, where he parked in front. Mona and his sister eyed him in patient silence. Taking the hint, he got out of the car and raced to the other side to assist Tiffany and Mona with dignified exits from the vehicle.

I swear they're communicating telepathically.

"Thank you, Joel," they said nearly simultaneously.

Tiffany led their column to the front door, where she knocked politely. Their father opened the door with a smile which faded quickly when he caught sight of Mona's green skin. Joel remembered his father as a strong man growing up, but his bulky strength was slowly sloughing into a pronounced paunch.

"Hi, Dad," Tiffany greeted him with a hug. "You remember my best friend, Mona."

"Hi, sweetie." With a curt nod, he added, "Joel."

Joel resisted the urge to clench his fists at his father's rude lack of greeting to Mona. "Dad, this is my girlfriend, Mona." Two sets of shocked eyes flicked toward him, but his father stared resolutely out the door rather than acknowledge the orc standing beside him.

"You can't say such things, son. You're a married man."

"Dad, I'm not—" Mona laid a soft hand on his arm, and he dropped the argument.

Tiffany drew his father off while Joel hung everyone's coats in the closet.

"Thank you, Joel." Her face wore a soft frown, but her lilac irises glimmered at him.

"I'm sorry. I knew he was an asshole, but he shouldn't act as if you aren't even there."

He led her toward the kitchen, where he saw Tiffany staring at him with wide eyes. She shook her head, but Joel didn't understand what silent warning she tried to convey. Inside the kitchen, his mother stood at the stove, an apron draped across her stocky frame as she stirred the gravy. His father leaned against the counter with a vicious smirk on his face. Joel's blood went cold when he saw the final occupant in the room. Her blonde hair shone in the light, and one hand rested on her bulging belly.

"Joel," his father announced with a cruel sneer, "you didn't tell us we were going to be grandparents."

"It probably isn't mine, is it, *Cheri?* Or, didn't she tell you it's probably her boss, Marc's child?"

"This baby *could* be yours," Cheri retorted.

"I doubt it. What are you doing here?" he asked, keeping a tight rein on his anger.

"Joel," his mother interjected in a hectoring voice, "that's no way to speak to your wife."

"She's not my wife. I signed the papers saying so."

He glanced at Mona. She gaped at his ex-wife with an expression of disbelief. Her stiff posture relaxed slightly when Tiffany put an arm around her.

"I didn't sign them, Joel. I'm still your wife, and I want to give us a real shot."

Joel stepped next to the woman he loved and took her jade green hand in his. "We already took our shot, and then you pissed it away. What happened, Cheri? Did Marc decide not to divorce his wife for you?"

His parents' heads turned to focus on Cheri. *Apparently she failed to mention everything.*

Cheri ignored his barb. "You know you'll never do better than me. I made a huge mistake with Marc, but I love you, Joel. Forgive me and I'll overlook your little roll in the gutter with an orc. Once you get checked for diseases, of course."

He barked out a derisive laugh. "Fuck off, Cheri. Mona has more class and wit than you could ever dream of. There's only one woman I can imagine the rest of my life with, and it sure as hell ain't you."

"Mona. *It* has a name." Cheri's face was twisted into a sneer, and Joel wondered how he ever thought she was beautiful.

He felt Mona's muscles quivering through their connected hands, but she didn't move. Instead, it was Tiffany who crossed the room in a flash and slapped Cheri's cheek.

Over the faint sounds of Cheri's shocked whimpers, Joel glanced quickly at Mona and nodded ever so slightly before he shifted his focus to his stunned parents. "Mom and Dad, choose now. Either she goes and we stay, or we walk out the door." He felt Mona's gentle squeeze of his hand and caught a slight nod from Tiffany.

"Joel, it's Christmas," his mother pleaded. "You can't throw a pregnant woman out at Christmas."

His father glared at Mona when he stated, "I won't share a table with one of them."

"Perfect, then we're leaving." He saw the faint glimmer of tears in Mona's eyes as he kept his grip on her hand as he led them toward the door.

Behind him, he heard Tiffany say, "I hope you two or three have a *lovely*"—her voice oozed sarcasm—"Christmas in this house that's as cold and soulless as your hearts." Her heels clicked down the hallway as she caught up to her best friend and brother.

Joel halted at the hall closet and retrieved their coats. Tears shimmered in Mona's eyes as he wrapped her coat around her shoulders. Knowing his parents and ex-wife were peering down the hall at them, he deliberately kissed Mona on her soft, warm lips. "I love you," he whispered as they parted.

As Joel ushered his girlfriend and sister out the door, his father's final words were, "Don't come back until you learn some sense, you filthy orc lover."

Unable to resist one last word, Joel craned his neck around to say, "Don't worry, pops. I won't."

Mona and Tiffany slid into the backseat where Tiffany cradled her friend in her arms as they cried together. Joel gripped the steering wheel as the adrenaline slowly faded from his blood.

"Back to Charity's place?"

Tiffany responded, "Oh hell, no. We didn't dress up like this for nothing."

He couldn't resist a wry chuckle. *I love my sister. She'll take good care of Mona for a bit. Meanwhile, I'll figure out what's open.*

After flipping through his map app, he found a likely spot. "Chinese work for y'all?"

"Heck, yeah. I could murder some Kung Pao right now. How about you, Mona?"

Mona's voice was brittle but bright. "Chinese sounds perfect."

"I'm on it." Joel started the car and drove off. He turned off the radio, unwilling to stomach the endless barrage of saccharine songs.

At a stoplight, Tiff tapped him on the shoulder. "Plug my phone in and hit play." He did as instructed, and Gloria Gaynor's *I Will Survive* blasted out of the speakers. "This is my girl power playlist. It seemed appropriate." Joel grinned as the light changed to green.

He waited patiently once they were parked at the restaurant for Mona and Tiffany to touch up each other's makeup. Once the damage from their tears was cleaned away and they felt presentable, the trio exited the vehicle. Inside, Tiffany asked the hostess for a table for three while Mona leaned her head onto Joel's shoulder.

She asked quietly, "Thank you. Are you okay?"

Joel's mouth gaped. "Seriously? My parents treated you horribly, but you're asking me if *I'm* okay?" He kissed her forehead. "I've got a lot going on, but I'll be fine. You're my only concern. How are you?"

Her fingers gripped his bicep firmly while her other hand held his hand. "I'm used to shitty people and mindless bigotry. It still hurts sometimes, but I have thick skin. You were the one who was ambushed by your parents and ex-wife, or is she still your wife?"

"Honestly, I don't know. It never occurred to me that she might not sign the divorce papers. I guess she didn't have complete faith in Marc after all."

They were interrupted when the hostess led them to their table. Joel felt the inquisitive stares of the few patrons as he walked arm-in-arm with Mona. A couple of the looks seemed disapproving, but he ignored them.

Mona shed her coat before she sat down primly.

"Have I told you how stunningly beautiful you are?"

She flashed him a fangy grin. "Not often enough."

"I'll do better, then."

"Damn right you will," Tiffany agreed. "Also, you two are disgustingly cute together. Our mom and dad suck, by the way. I'm sorry for how they treated you. I'll gladly trade close-minded parents for having a sister." She reached across the table to grasp Mona's hand. "You have always been my sister, no matter what your relationship is to this dumb oaf."

"Thank you, Tiff. You're my sister, too." Mona's lips curled into a wicked grin. "I'm glad *you're* smart enough to have never dated either of *my* brothers."

The two of them laughed, while Joel perused the menu and pretended to ignore the jibes at his expense.

"What were you two whispering about earlier?"

"We were talking about Joel's wife or ex-wife." Mona shifted to look at him. "What will you do if the kid is yours and not what's-his-face's?"

Joel let the menu fall listlessly from his hands. "Well, I'm pretty sure Marc is the father. On the off chance I'm the kid's dad, then I'm not entirely sure. One thing I do know is I'm not going back to Cheri. Nor am I moving back to Phoenix."

He could see Mona's shoulders straighten and light drift back into her eyes as if a heavy burden was lifted. Shifting to face her, he rested a hand on her knee and stared into her lavender eyes. "Mona, I don't know what the future holds for us, but I know I want there to be an *us* in it."

"You keep talking about a future, but I've never allowed myself the luxury of considering any kind of future with someone else. Especially not a human."

"I know I contributed greatly to your outlook, and I'm sorry. You deserve joy in your life."

She rested a green hand against his cheek and softly stroked him. "You do, too."

"Okay, before I blow chunks in my mouth, have you two figured out what you're going to order?" Tiffany's delighted expression didn't match her question. She winked at him to convey her approval.

They quickly perused their menus and were ready to order by the time the waitress arrived. After they ordered, Joel asked his sister, "Are you truly okay with us? I know you wanted to sleep with Mona."

"You're such an idiot, Joe-Joe. I would do anything for her, and I know she would do anything for me." She paused. "Mona, why do you look like you're about to die?"

"I told him about the birthday threesome."

"With Evan? *Damn, girl.* Way to be honest."

"Evan, right. I'd totally forgotten his name."

Tiff snickered, "I would have, too, except he was one of my better boyfriends."

"You have truly awful taste in men."

"Truth. I'd fully commit to dating women, but sadly, the best woman I know is apparently off the market now."

"Aww, you're sweet." Mona blew her friend a kiss.

"Anyway, Joe-Joe, to answer your question, I'm ecstatic for you both. I only wanted to help her out when she had a bad day. Of course, it would have been the best sex she ever had, so I guess she'll just have to settle for you."

"Joel does all right."

Tiffany put her hands to her ears and squeezed her eyes shut. "Nope, I don't want to hear about sex with my brother."

"What do you mean by 'all right'?" Joel asked.

"Oh, shush. Both of you. And thank you. You didn't have to leave your parents' house because of me."

"I can't speak for Tiff, but I didn't leave our parents' place only for you. I left for myself as well. They have manipulated and criticized both of us our entire lives. I give Tiff a lot of credit for standing by you her whole life despite them. She's always been stronger and better than me. I'm not going to put up with their shit anymore. Same with Cheri. If I'm the father, then I'll figure something out because I'm not going to abandon my kid, but I'm not going to let her weasel her way back into my life anymore than absolutely necessary, either."

"I'm happy to hear you are willing to step up if the baby is yours."

She looks like she wants to say something more, but lunch is here. Maybe we need to talk about something lighter for a bit.

"Are you going to share your Kung Pao, sis?"

"Of course I will, so long as you share your General Tso's, bro."

"Quit squabbling, you two. There's enough for all of us to share."

As Joel dug a spoon into the Kung Pao to maneuver it onto his plate, he asked, "Where'd you find those dresses?"

Tiffany glanced down at her clothes, then up at him. "Rosalinda, a friend of mine who is a costume designer, let me borrow them. She used to make outfits for me when we danced at the same club."

"Oh, right. I remember Rose," Mona said. "How is she?"

"She's great. Making a fortune designing costumes for drag queens."

"Good for her. I'm glad she had something in my size."

Tiffany giggled. "She designs clothes for drag queens. Of course she had something in *your* size. I'm about the same size as an actress on a TV show she's working on, so I'm lucky she had something for me."

This feels right. The three of us sitting around and having a good time. I don't feel good about leaving my parents behind, but life feels better without Dad's negativity and Mom's enabling. This is the family I want.

Chapter 18

Closer

Tegan and Sara

Mona felt Joel's eyes glued on her back all the way from the car to the door. The almost physical presence of his stare accelerated her heart and sent electric tingles skittering across her skin. She added an extra sway to her step, just as Tiffany had taught her to do so many years ago. Not the exaggerated swagger of a pole dancer, but the subtle touch of a courtesan. Her best friend noticed and cast an approving wink in her direction.

She smirked at his slack-jawed admiration as she stepped aside to allow him to unlock the door. Seized by a frisky fancy, she grasped Joel's ass and gave it a playful squeeze. His shocked hop elicited giggles from the two women.

He opened the door with a rueful shake of his head, but any trace of a frown was wiped from his face when she shed her coat and strutted over to him. She ran a polished nail under his chin before planting a quick kiss on his lips.

Tiffany coughed politely. "I need to change before I head off to the club. Please don't get any stains on the dress, or Rosalinda will have my head."

Joel looked toward his sister. "Will there even be any customers tonight?"

"It'll be a light night, but anyone at the club is likely to be lonely and desperate, which often means willing to spend money."

Mona felt a surge of anger and worry. "Stay safe and keep an eye on Gus. He's liable to turn a blind eye to handsy customers on a slow night."

"I know." Tiff planted a light peck on Mona's cheek. "I've got you on speed dial if shit hits the fan."

"You better. I will bust in there and break every neck in the club to keep you safe." The image of punching Gus in his smug face brought a wicked grin to her lips.

"I love you, too, Mona."

"Love you, Tiff." They embraced briefly before Tiffany darted off to change.

Whirling back to Joel, she planted a finger squarely in the center of his chest. "And you, mister. Why are you still standing there with leftovers in your hands?"

"Good call," he said with a sheepish shrug.

She cast an admiring glance at Joel's butt before she took advantage of his back being turned. Mona reached inside her dress and peeled off the boob tape before surreptitiously throwing it away.

Some secrets a man doesn't need to know. He already thinks my tits are magical, so why ruin the illusion?

"Hey, babe. Want to watch more cheesy Christmas movies?"

He straightened up and closed the refrigerator door before answering. "Nah. You can, if you want. I think I want to read some more, but I'll happily snuggle with you while you watch."

"Perfect." She set herself down gingerly on the couch so as to not wrinkle the dress and picked up the remote. "Can you grab my book from the bedroom as well, once Tiff is done?"

"Sure. Want any popcorn?"

"You read my mind."

"Anything to drink? Water? Hot chocolate? Tea?"

"Water is good for now. Thank you."

Tiffany popped her head over the back of the couch a few minutes later. "I'm heading out. You two have—ew." Tiffany made a disgusted face. "All the sleazy things I usually say just seem gross when I know you're banging my brother."

Mona chuckled. "Sorry, Tiff."

"You're not sorry at all, slut." Tiffany laughed and gave her a kiss on the cheek. "Don't worry. I'm just glad it's you and not that Cheri bitch. Joe-Joe may be an idiot, but he's still my brother, and I love him. I love you, too. And since you two are *finally* together, I don't have to be mad at him anymore. So, thank you, my green sister."

"Thank you for making this weird."

Tiffany smiled brightly as she replied with slightly manic cheer, "You're welcome."

"Also, you can't call me slut anymore. I'm a one-man orc now."

"Ugh, fine." Tiff pouted, then squealed, "I'm so happy for you."

"Me too." Mona turned serious. "Remember to call me if you need anything, hon."

"Will do. Bye, Joe-Joe."

Joel walked into the room, books in hand. "Later, sis." He paused and his face turned a rosy shade of pink. He added awkwardly, "Uh, strip well."

Tiffany looked Mona in the eye. "See, now he's making it weird."

The best friends blew each other kisses, and then Tiffany was gone. Mona patted the couch beside her hip. "Come sit with me."

"Did I say something wrong?"

"Dude, you told your sister to take her clothes off well."

"Yeah. I felt kind of icky the moment I said it." He set their books down on the small table. "I'll be back with the drinks and popcorn."

She picked up the remote and started scrolling through the choices of holiday romcoms, but each flick of her thumb seemed to deliver a feeling of something missing.

"Find anything?" Joel asked as he plopped down beside her and picked up his book. He felt warm and solid pressed against her flank.

"Not yet."

I want a happy, sugary escape from reality. A movie where someone who looks like me has a loving and supportive family and finds their happy ending. Instead, I have parents who have always prioritized my brothers. I have a new boyfriend, which is hopeful, but his parents hate me, and he's already left me once because of them. Why are there no movies where the nice, lonely orc girl finds her perfect match? Each movie I look at only makes me feel worse.

"Hey. Are you okay?" Joel asked.

"I'm fine. Read your book."

"Are you sure?"

"Yes. I don't want to bother you while you're reading."

Joel flipped a page, then flipped back. "I have a page and a half left in this chapter. When I finish it, you'll have my undivided attention."

She continued to scroll through movie choices as her mood turned evermore sour.

"I'm done. Would you like to talk?"

Mona grunted noncommittally as she thumbed the remote.

"Okay. Maybe not talking, though. I guess I'll just have to cuddle with you until you break." He rolled onto his side to rest his chin on her shoulder. One arm was thrown across her belly like a warm, heavy, and somewhat hairy belt. "I can see your boobs," he purred.

"*Joel.*"

"What? They're soft and green and enticing and right in front of me."

"You don't mind if they're green? Are you sure you wouldn't prefer another color?"

"Mona, I like your sweater puppies because they are yours." He lifted his hand off her stomach and brought it up to pull her chin over to face him. "I'm not going to feed you any 'I don't see color' bullshit. We both know it would be a lie. Your skin color matters to me—not for some fetish reason, but because it's part of who you are."

She rolled on her side to face him. "Your parents hate me. At the same time, part of me would feel guilty if your relationship with your parents was ruined."

"Yeah, well…" He stopped speaking and just stared at her for a while, and it felt sweet. "My relationship with them is not your fault. It's entirely my choice. I'm learning a lot about my parents, and I don't like it. The way my father treated you today—"

Mona choked back a sob as a tear rolled from her eye onto the bridge of her nose. Joel wiped it with a soft touch of his thumb. "—I'm furious with him. It's not only how he treated you as if you weren't there. He's been like this for his whole life, but I'm finally beginning to understand the depths of how miserable and hateful he's always been. Orcs, other humans, gay people: he loathes anyone who is somehow different from him. He hates them even more if they're happy. Dad is an awful person, and I don't need his negativity in my life."

"What about your mother?"

"Mom either agrees with him or she enables him. Either way, it's not healthy. I'd rather be with you and Tiff than them."

Mona closed in and held Joel tightly as she cried. He stroked her hair, wiped her tears, and cooed softly in her ear. The flow of tears eventually subsided, and she lifted herself onto one elbow. "I got you all wet. I'm so sorry."

"It's okay."

"You're staring at my tits, aren't you?"

Joel swallowed guiltily. "Yes." He lifted his gaze to meet hers. "Didn't Tiff say something about stains on the dress?"

Mona sat bolt upright and frantically searched the dress for wet spots. "Did I? I don't think…"

His facial expression was as innocent as an angel when he said, "You may want to take it off just to be safe."

She laughed as she smacked his arm, eliciting a wince. "*You pig. I'm crying my heart out, and all you care about is getting me naked.*"

He rubbed his bicep but still grinned. "Technically, you're no longer crying. Also, I feel like I'm simply being practical."

"Since I got you all wet, you should probably lose your wet clothes as well."

"You make a fair point."

They both stood, grinning like fools. Mona waited for Joel to pull his shirt over his head before she slipped a hand under one of her shoulder straps. She inched the strap slowly over her shoulder until it dangled uselessly on her arm. With one hand, she held her dress up while the other pointed at Joel's pants, and she wiggled her fingers to suggest he do something about his current state of dress. He doffed his pants with alacrity, at least until one leg caught on his heel, and he danced around while he pulled it off.

He flashed her a proud and lopsided smile as he stood with his pants gripped in his hand like he just won first prize. She answered his grin as she skimmed off the other shoulder strap. Mona held the dress up to her chest, building tension for the big reveal with the certain timing of someone who has absorbed the patterns of thousands of strip routines. Joel was practically quivering in anticipation, his eyes hungry as his tongue wantonly traced his fevered lips.

She let the edge of the dress dip, keeping her nipples fully covered but exposing the crested mounds of her breasts. Joel let loose an involuntary whimper in reply. Her dress dipped slightly lower as she fluffed her hair.

"Mona, you're killing me."

"What?" She batted her eyelashes innocently. "Oh, you mean my dress?"

"*Yes.*"

She dropped enough of the dress to fully expose one breast when Joel decided he'd had enough. He dropped his pants and stepped in to kiss her with the ferocious craving of a starving man. His body molded to hers as his mouth sought to feast upon her lips and tongue.

Mona melted into his kiss, forgetting about the dress, the television, and almost her name. Once her soul was satiated, she nudged Joel back and let the dress drop to the ground. She stood in front of him clad in only a black thong and let his vision drink her like a tall glass of water.

"Are you ready to read again?" she teased.

"Or something else."

"Down, boy. You'll get to taste me later. For now, I'd like to snuggle."

She lay back on the couch and settled in. He quickly joined her, his smooth, warm skin pressed against her. Mona marveled at how Joel's tanned skin contrasted with her own emerald green, reminding her of the verdant forests of Oregon. His pinky finger sidled against her thigh, sending shivers of delight through her rapidly moistening garden.

He laid his book on his chest and surveyed their bodies. "This couch is great. We should get one for our new place."

"*Our* new place?"

Joel sat up and drew up his legs as he twisted, fully focused on her. "Mona, move in with me. I'm looking for places. Wherever it is, come with me."

"What did I tell you about white knight bullshit?"

"I'm not trying to save you," he pleaded. "You've made it perfectly clear you can handle your own business. These past few days have been the best of my life. Look me in the eye, and tell me you don't feel it, too. If you don't, then I'll drop it and never bring it up again."

This is foolish. We've been snowed in for most of the last week, which isn't normal. None of this is normal. Then again, my shithole basement apartment is cold, damp, and generally sucks. Even if things don't work out with Joel, at least I'd have heat for a while.

And, he's not wrong. Whatever this madness is between us, I haven't felt this alive in a long time.

"Okay, but you're buying the couch."

Joel tackled her, burying her in grateful kisses. His unbridled enthusiasm soon slid into heated passion. She nipped at his ear as he ducked into to suckle her neck.

Goddess, he feels good. His skin pressed against my nipples is quickly destroying my ability to think.

With a grunt, she pushed him off her body. They could both tell by the pointed state of nipples and the bulging tent in his boxer briefs exactly how excited they were.

"I'm sorry, Mona. I got carried away, and there's no excuse."

"Oh, hush, you dimwit. If I'd wanted to stop you, I could have at any time. As it is, now I'm feeling cold. Throw a blanket over us and let's huddle up for warmth."

"As you wish."

Any inklings for getting frisky under the blanket were soon dashed by an invasion of cats. Muffy occupied Joel's lap while Chad curled up next to Mona's head and snored quietly in her ear. Itsabella futzed with the blanket near their feet until Joel lifted a leg to create a cave for Bitsy to enter. She then settled down by their feet and went to sleep.

Mona picked up the remote in one hand to find a movie while she rubbed Joel's head with the other.

"You still like the chrome dome look?" he asked.

"I love it."

Two cheesy holiday romcoms later, the cats began their evening pre-feeding routine of chasing each other wildly around the apartment. Joel groaned when Muffy left his lap to pursue Chad. "She's so heavy after a while."

"Why didn't you move her?"

"She looked so happy. I didn't want to disturb her."

"Softy."

Joel's head rotated on his neck at a dramatically slow pace until he faced Mona. "Oh, like you're one to talk. Anytime Itsabella hops in your lap, you're suddenly as soft as melted ice cream." He punctuated his critique by skimming his hand across her tummy to grip her waist.

"Down, boy. We need to feed the cats before they eat each other."

"Fine, but after they're fed, I want an appetizer."

"What were you thinking of eating?" Mona asked in a husky tone.

Joel leaned in so his breath brushed her ear like a feather when his deep, throaty voice whispered, "Your hot, soaking wet, delectable pussy."

I'm definitely dripping now.

"It's about time you used your tongue for something worthwhile."

"You're going to get a tongue lashing for your insolence, you saucy vixen."

A giggle leapt unbidden from her lips. "Why not just call me a wench?"

He rubbed his chin thoughtfully as he paused to consider her words. "You're right. Wanton wench would be much better than saucy vixen."

She dragged a fingernail down his jawline as she teased, "You can use your tongue to lap up my special sauce straight from the pot."

Joel chuckled. "Okay, you win the euphemism wars. Now let's feed some cats."

Mona felt the warm glow of victory, although she acknowledged it could easily be the heat of anticipation for Joel's tongue. The pair extricated themselves from the couch and fed the cats. As they monitored the feasting to ensure each cat ate from their own bowl and didn't bully another feline for food, Mona surreptitiously checked out the ample bulge in Joel's boxer briefs. Once the cats settled in for their post-dinner grooming, Joel took Mona's hand to lead her back to the couch.

She sat down and settled back to leer at him as he settled on his knees in front of her.

"May I finish undressing you and eat you out?"

"Fuck yes. You have my permission to make me scream like a banshee."

"I'll do my best." He slithered his hands up her thighs with the deliberate pace of a python binding fear-frozen prey. Firm fingers lifted the front of her thong, which Joel trapped in his teeth before his touch circumnavigated her taut and quivering ass cheeks. She lifted her hips to aid him as he languidly removed her final bit of clothing.

When her feet fell once again to the floor, she observed his beatific smile as he drank in her naked visage. Strong hands hooked under her thighs and yanked her forward so the V of her crotch was just over the edge of the seat.

"Comfortable?"

"Yes, but let me prop myself on some pillows. I want the boxed seats view when you're gorging yourself on my box."

"As you wish, my orc queen."

He waited until she was propped up before kissing her inner thighs. The slight hint of stubble on his chin tickled her sensitive flesh. She squirmed as he teased her with licks, nibbles and caresses just short of her aching pussy. Mona bucked her hips, silently urging him to finish the journey to where she desperately desired him to be, but Joel showed no inclination for haste. His wide, flat tongue left glistening trails upon her moss-colored skin, lubricating the ultra-fine sandpaper of his trailing chin.

"Damn it, don't stop," she commanded, but stop Joel did. Mona peered at him through heavy eyelids as he studied her intently. "What is it?"

"I'm fascinated by how stunningly sexy and gorgeous your pussy is."

"You like it?"

"I *love* it. I'm obviously biased and can't claim a vast breadth of experience, but you may have the prettiest pussy in the world."

She felt her ear tufts quivering. "You're only flattering me."

"No, I'm not. I love the subtle shift in the shade of your green skin as I approach your perfect lips."

Mona snorted. "One guy I dated called them beef curtains. Another said he preferred neat, tucked in labia because mine looked like a sandwich the whole city had a bite from."

"Those guys are idiots." Joel looked appalled. "Your lips make me imagine palm fronds sheltering a lush and inviting oasis from the harsh world outside or verdant petals surrounding a perfect blossom."

"I like your viewpoint better."

"Good." He flashed a wink which was equal parts sassy and smutty before he inhaled her lower lips into his mouth. He suckled and nibbled while his tongue probed and pleased inside and out.

Mona whimpered as tiny explosions sent sensual shockwaves racing from her toes to her brain. Joel released his sucking grip to switch to long strokes of his tongue sliding along her happy petals to her clit. She cried out as the tip of his tongue connected and circled before he dropped down for another long lick. He was eating her like she was the world's sloppiest ice cream cone, and her body responded.

Sweat beads popped across smooth green skin from her forehead to her trembling thighs. She clutched her hardened nipples, pinching and twisting them while Joel kneaded her ass like he was at a sourdough bake-off. Mona arched her back in an effort to press his face deeper into her aching center.

Joel didn't take the invitation. Instead, he switched to alternating long broad strokes of his tongue on her clit with pointed circles and figure eights. One hand retreated from her butt to slide one, then two, then three fingers inside her molten core. He pumped in and out in time with the worshipful ministrations of his tongue.

Mona tried to watch him, but her head kept flopping back as yet another tremulous tsunami of pleasure battered her beleaguered brain. At last, she couldn't take any more and gripped his smooth skull with iron-strong fingers and forced him to clamp his mouth down on her. He bit gently down around her clit while his tongue continued to swirl and lash, and Mona screamed her approval. Joel's fingers scissored and caressed the underside of her clit through the walls of her pussy.

The sensations inside and out drove Mona to writhe and wail until she exploded in an ecstatic supernova. Her heels drummed on Joel's back as she screamed her way through her orgasm. Her body fell slack as the shockwaves subsided.

Joel rose and wrapped her in his arms. He held her through the aftershocks until she raised her weary head to kiss his glistening face.

"I taste good. You're proud of yourself, aren't you?"

He smirked at her. "A little."

"As much as I hate to admit it, you deserve to feel some pride." Amidst the warm glow of her post-orgasmic haze, a slight chill crept into her psyche. "Can I admit something to you?"

"Of course."

"I'm starting to feel hope." Mona took a deep, calming breath. "A tiny sliver of a fantasy about a future with another person in my life."

Chapter 19

Still Loving You
Scorpions

"Wow. Thank you for opening up to me." Joel felt a combined surge of elation and terror which belied his calm and measured demeanor. Mona was handing him an opportunity to talk about their future, whereas before she'd shut him down.

Don't screw this up. Make good choices and be respectful. Be honest with her and yourself. You can do this.

"I'm processing your words so I can respond meaningfully." He paused for a breath and a sly smile. "I'll admit, my first reaction was to find this other person in your life and break their kneecaps."

She giggled, a sound he found thoroughly enthralling. "It's you, silly."

"It took me a minute, but I figured it out." He traced a fingertip along the lines of one of her tattoos. "Seriously, though, I want a future with you more than anything in the world."

"Why me? We barely know each other."

Where is this coming from?

"Mona, I've known you since you were six. We practically grew up together, although you were just my sister's annoying friend most of the time."

She stuck her tongue out at him. "Until I wasn't."

Joel rested his head on the couch cushion and gazed into her eyes. "I don't remember the moment you transformed from irritating pest to enchanting beauty, but one day I realized you weren't just a smartass but were smart as well. In our fifteen years apart, you have only become wiser, wittier, and even more beautiful."

"Flatterer."

He shrugged. "Call it what you want. Spending time with you quickly reinforced how amazing you've always been combined with how much you've matured over the years." His fingers stopped their tracing so he didn't distract Mona from what came next. "I fell in love with you all over again."

"Damn it, Joel. Why do you insist on making it sound so easy?"

Joel leaned in to kiss her. "What's easier than falling in love?" he whispered.

She snorted. "Falling is easy. Staying in love is hard work, especially once you realize all the shit that comes with loving an orc."

"I don't want you to think I'm downplaying anything you've told me. You've been very clear about the obstacles ahead." He ran his finger along her jawline before he cupped her cheek. "Today, I had a choice between you and my parents, and I chose you. There's going to be more of those decisions ahead of me, although it's difficult to say how many of them will be more challenging than cutting my parents out of my life at freaking Christmas. Living the rest of my life with you isn't going to be a walk in the park, but it's everything I want."

"You keep babbling about the rest of your life—what do you mean?"

Joel began tracing her tattoos again while he considered her question. *How do I answer this without scaring her off or coming across as out of touch? With honesty, obviously.*

"I'm not entirely sure what the rest of my life looks like. My head—like the future—is muddied and uncertain, but my heart is crystal clear. I can't predict what tomorrow will bring, but I want to be with you when it arrives. And then the next tomorrow..."

"You're not answering my question. Are you envisioning marriage, kids, a house with a white picket fence, and a minivan in the garage?"

He let a shudder pass through his body. "I'm feeling snakebit by marriage at the moment, but clearly Cheri was not the best choice for me, either. In retrospect, we got married because it seemed like the logical next step. Like some kind of Stepford life plan of marriage, house, kids, soccer practice, *et cetera.*"

Mona's eyes narrowed. "Speaking of kids, how do you feel about having kids, especially as you might already have one on the way?"

"I wasn't terribly enthusiastic, which I feel became a stress point with Cheri. I remember feeling a bit excited when she told me she was pregnant, and then a mixture of relief and anger when she told me it was Marc's. Relief it wasn't mine, although who knows, there's a small chance it could be. Anger mostly at her infidelity but also a bit at the lost opportunity. Now, I'm just confused."

Her expression isn't giving anything away. I hope I'm not sabotaging myself.

He continued, "I believe I could be a good father, but I've never felt this overwhelming urge to have children. I know raising kids is a life goal for some people, and that's great for them. It doesn't have to be everyone's goal, and I think I would be okay if I never did. Then, I also consider the future of any children we would have together. They'd be legally orcs and thus denied certain fundamental rights, which inspires me to want half-orc children as a symbol of defiance, but the logical part of my brain reminds me of how selfish such a choice could be."

"So?"

Joel blew out a heavy breath. "I'd prefer not to have kids, but if we did because of contraception failure or whatever, then I would love our child or children with all of my heart."

Mona laughed softly through her smirk. "You couldn't have just led with that?" She waved her hand in mock offense. "*No.* You had to drag me through your entire thought process. Plus, now I get to think of you banging your bimbo ex-wife." She stuck her tongue out and shuddered in disgust.

"We both have—"

"—pasts. I know. Anyway, I'm sure you're dying to know my opinion on progeny."

He nodded enthusiastically.

"I am exactly where you are. I've lived through enough discrimination in my own lifetime, and I wouldn't wish to burden a child with such a cruel fate. If we did have a kid, then I would fight like hell for her right to be whoever she wanted to be."

"How do you know we'd have a girl?"

Mona snorted. "Because I'd obviously want to raise the smartest, strongest child possible, so of course I would have a girl."

"I would be proud to raise a daughter who was as brilliant as her mother."

"Aw." Mona patted him gently on the cheek. "Maybe you aren't as dumb as you look."

"*Hey.*"

"I'm teasing you, silly."

He sniffed to show his wounded feelings before speaking. "Anyway, back to the question at hand. Our house would *not* have a carefully mowed lawn and a white picket fence. I'm thinking of a garden with only native plants."

"*Or,* we could live in a condo with a screened in deck where we could sit and sip coffee under a warm blanket while Itsabella looks at the birds before she burrows under the blanket to snuggle with us."

"Counterpoint, our house could have a deck or porch to do the same thing."

"True. What kind of house are you envisioning? Some giant Mc-Mansion?"

"Actually, I was picturing a cute little cottage with enough space to host small gatherings with my sister and our friends. Maybe a little upstairs bedroom for us—"

"And a sex dungeon in the basement," Mona exclaimed, her eyes dancing with feverish glee.

Joel forced his jaw closed before he responded. "*Wow.* Not where my mind was going at all, but sure, maybe we could have a shed for my workshop to free up space for an underground sex grotto."

"I was teasing about the sex dungeon. Mostly." She shrugged innocently. "What? Sometimes a girl has needs."

"To be tied up?"

"Who said anything about me being the one tied up and spanked?"

Joel chuckled to hide his nervousness. "Mona, you're killing me."

"You're a good boyfriend, Joel. You can have the basement for your workshop." She paused to grace him with a slow wink and a fangy grin. "We'll talk later about joining a sex club. I know a classy one which allows orcs to play."

"Do I want to know?"

"Blame your sister. I went there with her and her boyfriend for the threesome I told you about."

"You mentioned the threesome, but somehow failed to mention *where* you had it. Were people watching you when you...you know?"

"Did people watch us? Oh yeah. We attracted quite a crowd. Your sister is gorgeous, and I'm obviously stunning."

"*Obviously.*"

"Thank you. And honestly, her boyfriend could have been Quasimodo for all anyone cared, but he was decent looking." Mona bit her lower lip and moaned. "Of course, he wasn't nearly as hot as you." She rubbed his shaved head, then shivered and squirmed. "Oh damn, Joel. You and I could put on one hell of a show."

"I'm not sure I'm up for public sex."

Mona's smile softened. "If you're not, then we never have to do anything. I would like to take you to the club once. We don't have to do anything."

"I've never been to a sex club before."

"You're curious, aren't you?" She smirked at him, her violet eyes glittering in impish delight.

"A little."

Her hand slithered under the blanket to grasp his pulsing package. "I'll wear something jaw-droppingly sexy just for you. Everyone in the club is going to want to fuck me silly, but I will only allow you to touch me." Mona licked his jaw up to his ear, then growled in his ear, "if anyone else tries to lay a finger on me, I'll break their arms."

He groaned. Her fingers teased him to rigid attention, drawing forth further whimpers from his throat.

"You enjoy thinking of me as your personal fucktoy, don't you?"

"I mean...I think of you as much more than merely a fucktoy, Mona."

She rolled her eyes as she leaned in to kiss him. "Stop trying to be noble and considerate while I'm seducing you." Her lips locked onto his, her fangs scraping against his cheekbones as she slowly snogged him. Mona threw a leg over him, and Joel suddenly felt steaming soaked heat against the head of his steely shaft. "There's one more portion of the question to answer." She wiggled against him. "You want to answer correctly."

"What was the question again?" His voice sounded as desperate as his racing heart felt as it slammed against his sternum.

"Minivan?"

"Oh, fuck no. Maybe a hatchback. Never a minivan." His cock was immediately encased in teeming tropical heat.

"Good answer," Mona grunted as she slid down his shaft.

"My...pleasure," he panted in response.

Later, as their sweat-soaked bodies cooled in the afterglow of their frenzied exertions, Joel chortled. "You must hate minivans."

"They remind me of the unholy smell of football pads and un-washed boys. The stench of my parents' minivan is forever carved into my memory."

He nodded sagely. "Not something I ever experienced."

"I had two football-playing brothers. I wouldn't wish those foul fumes on anyone. Well. Almost anyone. Okay, fine. I can imagine quite a few people who should suffer such torment and worse."

"Remind me to never get on your bad side."

She sniggered. "Two weeks ago, you were a permanent fixture at the top of my shit list. You definitely would have been driving the minivan from hell. You're lucky you're still cute."

"Only cute?"

She shook her head while flashing him a wry grin. "And kind. Not a complete dumbass. Oh, and you introduced me to Itsabella."

"And?" He asked hopefully.

"Your dick is still inside me. Don't push your luck, Joel."

"Point taken."

239

"And?" He asked hopefully.

"Your dick is still inside me. Don't push your luck, Joel."

"Point taken."

Chapter 20

Taking Care of Business

Bachman Turner Overdrive

The next morning, Joel helped Mona write out a business proposal for a frozen treats shop. When they were done, he said, "It looks great, but I think you should do another."

"Why?"

"Have a backup plan in place. We've already acknowledged the difficulty in getting a loan you're likely to face. If we...you can't secure a loan for a brick and mortar shop, then a food cart could be your fallback option."

"No. I'm not doing it, Joel. I've been dreaming about a cozy little shop with a counter by the window and stools for people to sit on while they eat their ice cream or yogurt. I want a case where kids can press their noses against the glass to look at the flavors."

Mona felt her hackles rise when Joel chuckled. She calmed when he commented, "We're going to have to clean some kid's snot off the glass every day."

She sniffed at him. "It'll be worth it." Mona took his hands in hers. "My little shop is going to be a neighborhood staple where everyone is served with a smile. More than anything, I want orc kids to come into my shop and find hope for a better future for themselves. We're more than just the people who do the dirty jobs no one else wants to do. My shop is going to bring a bit more hope and joy into the world."

Joel smiled at her. "I apologetically retract my suggestion. Your shop is worth fighting for."

"No apology is needed. Honestly, I've toyed with the food cart idea for a long time. It would be easier and cheaper to start up, but once I made the decision to make my fantasy a reality and to open my shop, it no longer made sense. I'm going to dream big and bring my vision to life."

"I love you."

"I love you, too, dork."

"Dork? I'm not the big softie inside the hard, green tattooed shell."

Mona snickered. "You make me sound like a crab."

"I'm my defense, you can be pretty crabby in the morning until you get some coffee or tea."

"Or thick, hard cock."

Joel stroked his chin as he pondered her retort. "True, although I believe my statement is still correct as you do enjoy caffeine after cock."

"Smart ass." She couldn't contain the smile growing on her face. "You're lucky I tolerate your sass."

"Mona, I consider myself to be the luckiest man in the world. I have to pinch myself continuously to make sure I'm not dreaming."

"Again. You're such a dork." She squeezed his hands affectionately. "Let's grab some lunch and go to this place I think would be perfect."

"Of course." He leaned in for a quick kiss.

The next morning, he gave her hand a comforting squeeze before he opened the door to the bank. There was only one loan officer on duty two days after Christmas, and she took Joel first. Mona sat patiently in the lobby, ignoring the suspicious stares of the employees while she listened to cheerful laughter from the cubicle where Joel discussed his small business loan.

The smile slid off the loan officer's face when she ushered Mona into the cubicle for her turn. She grilled Mona relentlessly for nearly an hour, probed into every aspect of the business plan, Mona's financials, and legal history. There was no laughter.

In the end, the loan officer finally smiled when she denied Mona's application for a loan. Mona held her head stiffly as she stalked out of the cubicle.

I just want to get Joel home and hug him while I cry my eyes out and eat a gallon of ice cream. Fuck this bitch.

Joel stood before her in the lobby, his face as angry and mottled as a thundercloud. He looked at her and asked, "Sweetheart, may I?" Mona heard the subtle intake of breath behind her at the revelation of her relationship to Joel.

She nodded. "Yes."

He grinned with a wicked delight in his eyes. Joel pitched his voice to carry across the bank lobby. "Pardon me, Lisa. I'd like to speak with your manager about your inequitable treatment of my girlfriend."

"I'm not sure—"

"Bullshit. You know *exactly* what I mean. You skipped over basic questions for me, laughing and flirting the whole time."

"I wasn't flirting."

He snorted. "Yeah, you were. I've never met a banker who emphasized three times to call their cell phone if I need anything at all. Meanwhile, you treated Mona with cold disdain and asked intrusive questions well beyond the scope of what you needed to know to approve a loan. Questions you definitely did not ask me." Joel's volume was rising steadily, attracting the full attention of the few people in the bank.

"Some clients require additional scrutiny."

"Orcs," Joel growled. "You mean orcs get the third degree while humans get a pass."

"Your circumstances are different."

"Oh, I'm well aware."

"Excuse me, is there a problem?" The three of them wheeled as one to face a human woman in a dark suit. Her cool expression and assertive stance practically screamed "manager."

Joel smiled sweetly. "Yes, despite my long history with your bank, I believe I'll be taking my business elsewhere, including my personal accounts, given the discrimination I've witnessed against my girlfriend."

Mona stood her ground, pointedly not touching Joel, while she struggled with the emotions inside. *I'm angry Joel feels like he needs to intercede on my behalf, but mostly I'm pissed at this person for how she treated me. I feel humiliated, even though I expected it. Then again, Joel is putting himself out there for me, risking his own future. It's an attractive trait in a partner and what I was looking for.* Her skin felt clammy, and her armpits were soaked with sweat, but there was a countervailing warmth growing in her chest.

"My name is Kendall. Why don't we all sit down and review the documentation again? Perhaps there is something Lisa missed."

Lisa looked none too pleased about this turn of events, and Mona tried not to let her fangs show through her tight-lipped smile as Kendall ushered them all back into the cubicle. The bank manager perused the business plan, asking some pointed questions about the cost and revenue projections.

The manager interrogated Mona about her experience.

This is the hard part. I'm starting to feel like I'm banging my head against a wall, but I know it's necessary.

Mona explained how she worked summers at an ice cream shop in her teens. She observed the process for making ice cream and eventually was trained to make ice cream because the shop owner preferred having humans serving customers. In the intervening years, she'd researched new equipment and techniques, including liquid nitrogen cooling.

Apparently satisfied by Mona's answers, Kendall finally asked, "How certain are you regarding the location and building costs?"

Joel responded, "I have my real estate agent looking into a space on Hawthorne. Competition would be effectively non-existent, foot traffic would be excellent, and the price per square foot is within an affordable range. She's optimistic about our—sorry, Mona's chances."

The bank manager steepled her fingers. "I know full well this is a rude question, but does your agent or the building's owner know that Mona is an orc?"

He slumped back in his chair before saying, "No. They don't."

"Hmm. The proposal is excellent. I appreciate seeing conservative cost and revenue projections. Far too many people are wildly optimistic. We will approve a loan for this location. If the space cannot be secured, then we will re-evaluate based on new information. I will be happy to work with you personally." She looked Mona directly in the eyes. "I'm looking forward to trying your ice cream. If I might make a request, perhaps you could try out a dark chocolate peanut butter flavor."

"I would be happy to. Thank you so much."

Kendall stood and extended her hand. "Thank you for coming in today."

Mona shook her hand, responding, "I appreciate your assistance in re-evaluating my loan application."

"Happy to help."

Mona could see the deep frown on Lisa's face as her boss shook Mona's green hand. *Yeah, you racist bitch. Hate didn't win today.*

She slipped her hand into Joel's as they walked out of the bank together. "Thank you for making a scene."

"I was happy to use my privilege for good, but only with your permission, of course."

"It sucks that you had to use it at all."

"She did not treat you fairly, and certainly nowhere near how she treated me with all the laughing and flirting."

"You didn't want to ditch me for your new girlfriend, Lisa?" Mona asked with a teasing lilt in her tone.

He sighed and rolled his eyes. "She certainly seemed to like me—until she found out I was already dating a stunningly beautiful woman."

"Yeah, you are." She stopped to kiss him next to his car. "Seriously though, I'm glad you asked and didn't charge right in with some white knight bullshit."

"*See.* I am trainable."

Mona's eyebrows arched. "Debatable."

He pouted briefly before smiling broadly. "Want me to call my realtor? We could check out the shop."

"You wouldn't mind?"

"Not at all. I feel personally invested in your success now."

"*Only now?*"

Joel chuckled. "I've been all-in ever since I walked into my cabin and found you there."

"You're just saying so because I was naked."

He scratched his chin thoughtfully. "Naked is one of my favorite states of Mona."

She laughed as she smacked his arm. "Pervert."

"You love it."

"Yeah. I do. Now call your realtor. Afterward, we're going to see my tattoo artist. It's time to celebrate by getting you inked."

Joel gulped, but still nodded his assent.

Margot, Joel's real estate agent, did a double take when they walked up to her arm-in-arm, but if she harbored any bigoted opinions, she kept them to herself. "Hi, you must be Joel," she said, extending her hand. "It's nice to put a face to all of the emails and texts." After shaking Joel's hand, she focused on Mona, reaching out for another handshake. "And you must be Mona. I'm Margot. Lovely to meet you as well. Joel told me briefly about your froyo and ice cream shop plans. This is very exciting."

The woman's cheer was nearly overwhelming, but Mona was used to big personalities after bouncing at so many strip clubs and bars. "Good to meet you as well, Margot. How did you find Joel as a client?"

"Oh, he found me. My sister lives in Phoenix with her partner, and Joel rewired their entire house, new lighting, everything. He did a phenomenal job. Anyway, when he told her he sold his business to move to Portland, she gave him my name. Mike, my husband, wants to remodel our house, and I've been so-so about it, but with Joel in town, I've agreed to do it, but only if Joel works the same electrical magic he used on my sister's house."

"Magic, you say." Mona purred. "I was unaware of the scope of Joel's talents."

"Oh, yes. Mary's house is a wonder. So much brighter and lively now. If you don't mind, how long have you two been dating?"

Mona and Joel shared a glance before looking back to Margot. "Not long, but we've known each other since we were kids. His sister is my best friend."

"The best friend's brother?" The real estate agent waggled her eyebrows. "Delicious. Are you ready to check out the space?"

Mona felt a bit dizzy amidst the whirlwind of conversation, so she gladly took safe harbor in the agent's offer of the tour. "Yes, please."

"Wonderful. Ken is inside. He's the agent for the owner. Don't agree to anything without consulting me." Margot whirled and stepped briskly toward the door with Joel and Mona trailing slightly shell-shocked in her wake. Ken greeted them at the door before ushering them inside.

Mona marveled at the open space as her mind filled the gaps with stools, tables, and a line of customers. Ken led them into the back of the house area, and the sense of wonder faded rapidly. Ovens and a commercial griddle took up much of the cramped space. Dollars flashed burning scarlet in her mind about the amount of expense needed to convert this space into a creamery. Her blood ran cold when Ken discussed the price per square foot. It was within her range, but just barely.

"Joel," she whispered. "I can't."

"I think we can. Follow my lead."

"I trust you."

Joel stalked over to the walk-in refrigerator and opened the door. "Your offer isn't going to work, Ken. This fridge was built in the Eisenhower administration, and it shows. The electrical system is nearly as old, and I guarantee it isn't up to code. This is prime real estate on one of the busiest shopping streets in Portland, and it's been empty for what—"

"Sixteen months," Margot supplied.

"Everything back here needs an upgrade, and once you touch one thing, you'll have to bring *everything* up to code. I'm going to guess the owner doesn't want to pay the expense, and you can't find a renter willing to do it, either."

Ken's silence spoke volumes.

"You're going to give Mona six free months in exchange for bringing this mess up to code and stripping the old equipment out of here."

"Well, I—" Ken sputtered before Mona jumped in.

"And then you're going to get rid of the orc tax you tacked onto the rent amount. I looked through the paperwork Margot sent us this morning, and your asking price is above similar properties in this neighborhood. It's also *far* above what the previous tenant paid." Mona popped her fangs out as she grinned. "So, you're going to charge the market rate you would charge a human." He paused and grinned. "No. Actually, you're going to charge ten percent under market rate for insulting Mona in the first place."

Ken shook his head. "I'm sorry. I guess we don't have a deal then."

Mona nodded. "I'm sorry, too. We'll go check out our next choice, then." She slipped her arm into Joel's and turned on her heel. This time, Margot followed behind them as they exited the shop.

They'd already turned down the street when Ken called out, "Wait."

Gotcha. Always be willing to walk away. If they need it more, then they'll cave. I guess Ken feels he needs this more, although it's a good thing he doesn't know we don't have a backup plan right now.

"Four months free, we'll cover twenty-five percent of the renovation cost, and you'll get market rate on the price per square foot."

"Forty percent on the renovations and five percent under market rate," Margot countered.

The three of them stood on the frigid Portland sidewalk and watched Ken as he argued silently with himself before his shoulders slumped in defeat. "Thirty percent on the renovation and we have a deal."

Margot chuckled. "Not entirely, but I'll draw up the paperwork, and the two of us will hammer out the minor details."

"I look forward to hearing from you. Mona, congratulations in advance." Ken held out his hand, and she shook it. Mona resisted the temptation to squeeze extra hard as revenge for the price hike for her being an orc. Being the better person was hard sometimes.

"Thank you, Ken. I look forward to working with you."
No, I don't, but I'll be polite.

Margot snickered once Ken was out of earshot. "Remind me never to play poker with you two."

Chapter 21

Butterflies

MAX featuring Fletcher

Mona ran a rag across the glass one last time, just to be sure it was spotless. Tabletops gleamed in the late morning sun, napkin dispensers were stocked, and the topping containers were full. It was already warm outside, and the forecast for this mid July day was hot, so business was likely to be good.

She flipped the sign to read "OPEN" before she unlocked the door. The two girls standing on the other side of the door were bouncing on their feet in anticipation. One human, one orc, they held hands as they dashed inside the moment she opened the door. Their respective mothers brought up the rear, chatting idly as their daughters pressed their noses to the freshly cleaned glass. Mona recognized the human woman as Kendall, the bank manager who helped secure the loan half a year before, and flashed a friendly smile and nod.

Echo, her teenage employee, reached a green hand inside the display case to fill two tiny sample spoons and pass them to the girls. Joel hummed happily in the back as he made fresh waffles to be twisted into cones.

"You have to try the dark chocolate peanut butter ice cream," Kendall said to her friend. "It's to *die* for."

"Thank you," Mona interjected. "It's good to see you again."

Kendall nodded at her child. "This is Jenna's new favorite place, so I'll be here a lot."

"I'm so glad she loves my ice cream. Hey, sweetie," Mona called out to Joel. "Can you come out here for a minute?"

"Sure, love."

"Look who's here."

"Oh, hi, Kendall." Joel raised a freshly tattooed arm to greet their customers.

"Hey, Joel. I didn't know you worked here."

Mona giggled. "He doesn't. Joel likes to come in on Saturdays and Sundays to help out in the shop, and I'm always happy for the help. It gets busy in here, especially on weekends, and he's handy with waffles."

"He's a good boyfriend," Kendall replied.

"Not my boyfriend anymore," Mona grinned as she extended her left hand into the morning sunlight, where an amethyst gemstone set on a silver band sparkled.

Acknowledgements

Writing is an individual effort, but also a communal one. A book doesn't come to be without the support of a broad and supportive community. Thank you to everyone who has read one of my books. I hope you've enjoyed them.

Obviously, a huge thank you to my partner and editor, Cecily. Honestly, it was a gigantic leap of faith to have her become the primary editor for me, and she's been amazing. I appreciate her vision so much, and I enjoy being able to really talk things through. My writing is better because of it.

Much love to our cats, Merlin, Lady Starlight, and our beloved but departed Francesca. They each inspired bits of Itsabella's personality.

As always, thank you to my good friend, Steve Davala, for kickstarting me on the journey of writing. I never thought I'd write one book, and now I have six! Thanks, my friend!

Thank you to Priya and Mercy at the Books and Martinis podcast for having me on! Special shout out to Priya, who was so excited about the idea of Snow Ordinary Love that she got to read the first draft. I love your show, and keep introducing the world to great books and authors!

Cort, thank you for providing both an explanation and a demonstration of shaving someone's head.

Thank you to my beta readers, with a special shout out to Emma for some of the most detailed feedback I've ever seen.

To the writing community, thank you! To my online author friends, especially Loren and Stacey, much love to you! I've found a lot of support here in Portland, especially amongst romance writers and sci-fi/fantasy writers. Being an indie author isn't easy sometimes, and having a community of friendly people helps.

Speaking of, thank you to everyone who supports indie writers! Especially you if you've made it this far. I appreciate everyone who takes a chance on an indie author. Thank you.

About the author

Chris Walters is a romance author living in Portland, Oregon with his wife and two cats. When not reading, writing, or working his day job, he is an announcer for the Rose City Rollers. He self-published his first novel, No One Like You in 2024.

www.ingramcontent.com/pod-product-compliance
Lightning Source LLC
Chambersburg PA
CBHW020751310726
48969CB00002B/488